Two
Paradise

It was either Billy Druid's Blue on Blue, with its
soulful sax, or it was the way in which Mason
held her tightly in his arms which had made the
hairs on the back of Jackie's head stand to
attention. Maybe it was a combination of both.
They'd danced until their faces glistened with
sweat, but now, smooching around to this beautiful ballad, Jackie felt really . . . alive. She ran her
fingernails across the back of his wet, pale blue
shirt and felt him shiver as he pulled her even
closer. He bent forward and kissed her ear, lingering for a while before taking the lobe between his
lips. He brought his kisses down onto her cheek
and then gently, very gently, onto her mouth. She
felt her legs go weak as she responded to the long,
passionate kiss. And she told herself, Careful,
Jackie. Don't get carried away. This is just a
holiday romance!

Two Weeks in Paradise

Denise Colby

Cover illustration by Derek Brazell

■SCHOLASTIC

For Denis Bond

Scholastic Children's Books,
Scholastic Publications Ltd,
7–9 Pratt Street, London NW1 0AE, UK

Scholastic Inc.,
555 Broadway, New York, NY 10012-3999, USA

Scholastic Canada Ltd,
123 Newkirk Road, Richmond Hill,
Ontario, Canada L4C 3G5

Ashton Scholastic Pty Ltd,
P O Box 579, Gosford, New South Wales,
Australia

Ashton Scholastic Ltd,
Private Bag 92801, Penrose, Auckland,
New Zealand

First published by Scholastic Publications Ltd, 1994

Text copyright © Denise Colby, 1994
Cover artwork copyright © Derek Brazell, 1994

ISBN 0 590 55616 9

Typeset by TW Typesetting, Midsomer Norton, Avon
Printed by Cox & Wyman Ltd, Reading, Berks.

1

The plane was almost full as Jackie flopped into the window seat, grinning excitedly. She gently primped her red hair with her fingertips and turned to face Caroline.

"Who'd have thought it?" she said. "You and me in the Caribbean. I can hardly believe it."

The events of the past two months had taken the girls and their respective families by surprise. On leaving school Jackie had secured a plum job as a trainee sound-engineer in a recording studio whilst the blonde and extremely pretty Caroline, never as ambitious as her best friend, was soon to start work at the local supermarket. And that was just the *start* of their good fortune.

The stewardess approached slowly along the aisle of the plane, checking that all her charges had fastened their seat-belts.

"Have you noticed there're no kids on the plane?" whispered Jackie.

"Lacruz is too posh for kids," lectured Caroline,

who'd been talking to a friend of her mother who worked as a travel agent. "They say it's very expensive and only the rich go there: Joan Collins, Princess Diana . . . those sort of people."

Jackie sighed contentedly and repeated, "Who'd have thought it?"

Earlier in the year the two girls, sitting together at the back of the French class and oblivious to Madame Girard's pearls of wisdom, had half-jokingly filled in the competition in Jackie's copy of *Chartbusters*. The top prize was a place on London Weekend Television's teen quiz show, *Triangles*. To the shock and delight of all their friends, the girls had appeared on the show, sailed easily through to the final and had eventually won the star prize – Two Weeks In Paradise.

"Well, if it's that expensive," said Jackie, "I just hope LWT's given us enough spending money. Suppose we run out?"

Caroline shrugged. "Then we'll have to find some rich fellas to buy us drinks, won't we? There'll be plenty of 'em out there."

She looked round the plane, searching for the groups of single men. There were none. The travellers appeared to be mainly couples; just marrieds . . . just retireds . . . those obviously celebrating some kind of anniversary.

"What about those couple of rows of empty seats at the back?" queried Jackie. "D'you think a bus-load have got held up on the M25?"

Caroline looked at her watch. It was eleven fifteen.

2

"Looks like it," she said. "We should've taken off twenty minutes ago."

All heads suddenly turned to face the back of the plane as a group of noisy, young people scuffled in and was hastily directed to the empty seats by the stewardess.

Caroline counted. Ten men and two women. Ten young men. Ten good-looking, young men.

"Oh, yes," she sighed. "That'll do nicely."

Although both girls had travelled abroad before − Jackie to Tenerife and Caroline to Majorca − neither had realized how tiring a long-haul flight would be. Over ten hours travelling − eight of them in the air − which, Caroline had commented, was as long as two full days spent at school. As yet, they were only halfway through their journey.

"Not quite the same as school dinners though, is it?" smiled Jackie through a mouthful of chicken supreme. "I could live like this all the time."

"Hey! Talking about school," said Caroline, looking worried, "I've just had a horrible thought. What was our most hated subject in the whole wide world?"

"French!" laughed Jackie.

"Yeah, French! And what language do they speak in Lacruz?"

"Not French?" gasped Jackie.

"Yeah!" said Caroline.

Both girls screamed in mock horror.

"Oh, no!" giggled Jackie. "I mean ... mais non ... we won't be able to ask for anything!"

"We'll starve!" yelped Caroline.

"We'll have to eat patty-dee-foy-groy or what-ever they call it, *every day*!"

"And frogs' legs!"

"Ugh!" they both screeched before bursting into hysterical laughter.

The middle-aged couple sitting in the row in front of them, turned and glared.

"Please!" snapped the woman.

Jackie responded with a French accent, "Pardon madame!"

The woman turned back to finish her meal.

Caroline and Jackie looked at each other and covered their mouths with their hands to stifle their laughter. Jackie took her handkerchief from her pocket, rolled it into a ball and stuffed it into her mouth. Her body shook as tears rolled down her cheeks. This made Caroline worse. She could hardly speak for fear of letting out a high-pitched cackle.

A steward, pushing a trolley along the aisle, stopped and stared at Jackie.

"Are you all right?" he asked. "Do you feel sick?"

Jackie didn't feel sick. But she did feel silly! She removed the handkerchief from her mouth and mentally reprimanded herself for being so childish.

"No. I'm all right," she said. "Thank you."

The steward smiled and was about to leave when Jackie called to him. "Excuse me! Can you tell me what language they speak in Lacruz?"

"Spanish," he replied. "But nearly everyone speaks English, so there's no problem."

4

Jackie felt a little disappointed. "Thank you," she said. The joke was over.

Caroline was oblivious to the conversation; her mind elsewhere as she stared open-mouthed towards the back of the plane. She turned back to Jackie with an inane grin on her face.

"Did you hear what the steward said?" asked Jackie.

"No," replied Caroline as she grabbed Jackie's hand in a vice-like grip. "You'll never believe it!" she whispered.

"What?"

"You know that group that came late and sat at the back of the plane?"

"Yeah?"

"One of them's only . . ." she gulped.

"Only what?" asked Jackie.

She turned her head to stare at the group and immediately noticed the blond-haired, blue-eyed Irish heart-throb, number-one pop star . . . Duane Sheldon!

During the flight, Caroline had to leave her seat several times and as she sauntered to the back of the plane, she did her best to catch Duane Sheldon's attention. He was totally unresponsive to her smiles and spent the whole journey either watching the in-flight movie or chatting to the burly minder at his side. A couple of men in his entourage, however, had fired chat-up quips at Caroline as she wiggled seductively past their row of seats.

Jackie was curious to know what the famous

pop star looked like in the flesh but later, when she had to pass by his seat, she was too embarrassed to linger and only got a glimpse of his tousled, blond hair.

She found that both the toilets at the back of the plane were occupied and waited patiently, watching the stewards racing around in their cabin, preparing tea.

"Hi!" said a short, stocky lad with cropped hair and five-o'clock shadow. "Are they both engaged?" he mumbled through his chewing-gum.

"'Fraid so," replied Jackie.

He leaned back against one of the toilet doors and stared in at the busy cabin crew, giving a wink to one of the prettier stewardesses as she turned to place a tray of teacups onto a trolley.

"Business or holiday?" he asked Jackie, knowing the reply to his question.

"Holiday," she smiled. "You?"

"Business."

He waited for her to enquire further. She didn't.

"I'm with a film crew," he volunteered.

"Really?" She tried not to sound too impressed.

"Yeah. We're shooting a video on Lacruz."

Jackie felt there was no need for a response.

"A pop promo. With Duane Sheldon," he added.

He hadn't expected her to react quite so coolly. "Yes. I noticed he was on the plane."

"Nice bloke," he said. "I've worked with Duane quite a few times, actually. Not at all starry. Not like some of them."

His eye once again caught the eye of the stewardess. "All right, darling?" he asked, flinging the chewing-gum to the other side of his mouth.

She returned a flicker of a smile and continued with her work.

He put out his hand to shake Jackie's. "Pete," he said.

"Jackie," she replied.

"Have you been to Lacruz before?" he asked her.

"No. Have you?"

"Yeah. You'll love it. Paradise!"

One of the toilet doors clicked open and an elderly woman with blue hair emerged. Jackie allowed her to pass and then began to enter.

"By the way," said the lad, as if this were just an afterthought. "What's Blondie's name?"

"Caroline," replied Jackie, with a smile.

She went into the toilet and locked the door.

The plane landed thirty minutes later at Vega airport, six-fifteen London time. The natives and holiday-makers on Lacruz had just finished lunch. Jackie gasped as she stepped from the aircraft and felt the blanket of warm air smother her.

"I don't believe it," said Caroline. "It's like putting your head in the oven."

As they descended the steps towards the bus parked on the tarmac, the girls struggled out of their coats.

"What did we bring these for?" panted Caroline. "I can't wait to get my clothes off and get into the sea."

The bus transported them to the customs hall

where, as they waited for their luggage, Caroline chatted constantly to Jackie, her eyes never leaving Duane Sheldon's entourage. The crew picked up several large, metal boxes and dozens of pieces of camera equipment from the conveyor and piled them high onto the three trolleys which had been reserved for them.

"Oh, no! They're going," whispered Caroline in panic as she watched the men load their last piece of luggage and wheel the trolleys towards the sign marked *salida*. "Where's our flamin' luggage?" she snapped impatiently, eyeing the suitcases and zip-bags of all shapes and sizes circling round and round in front of them.

The representatives for Caribtours – one young man and one young woman, dressed in bright red and white uniforms – stood, clipboards in hand, at Vega airport's main lobby, ticking off the names of the weary, sweat-dampened travellers and directing them onto the coach which was to take them to their hotel.

Caroline and Jackie slumped into the front seats beside the handsome, black driver.

"Hot, isn't it?" Jackie grinned at him.

He grinned back, showing whiter-than-white teeth, but said nothing.

"He doesn't understand," whispered Caroline, keeping one eye on the window, hoping that she'd see Duane Sheldon heading towards the coach. "Try it in French. 'Chaud' isn't it?"

"There'd be no point," giggled Jackie. "They speak Spanish here."

"No. French," argued Caroline confidently.

"No," said the driver. "She's right. Spanish. And English. And yes . . . it's very hot!"

As the coach pulled away, Caroline suddenly gripped Jackie's arm. "Look!" she exclaimed as she peered through the window.

Duane Sheldon's men were packing the last of the metal boxes into one of two Land Rovers parked in the airport car-park.

"D'you think they're staying at the same hotel?"

"Of course not," replied Jackie. "We're just package tourists, aren't we? They'll be staying somewhere luxurious."

The coach travelled speedily along Lacruz's main, but almost empty, road . . . passing fields of sugar-cane and fruit trees. White villas, dotting the lush green hills all around, were covered in vibrant red and orange flowers and surrounded by tall palms. Jackie and Caroline were silent, gazing in awe at the cloudless, bright blue sky and longing to catch their first glimpse of the Caribbean sea.

The vehicle suddenly veered to the right and bumped its way along a narrow, pot-holed road, sending brightly coloured birds fluttering from the trees lining the route.

"What are they? Parrots?" screeched Jackie excitedly.

"Dunno," gasped Caroline. "Budgies, I think."

The driver laughed heartily as he manoeuvred the coach across a particularly uneven piece of ground, bouncing the passengers up and down in their seats.

Then Jackie noticed the large, white building ahead of them.

"Is that the hotel?" she asked the driver.

"The Club Maritimo. Yes," he replied.

"Where's the sea?" asked Caroline.

"On the other side of the club," grinned the driver.

Jackie began to worry. "I bet we have to cross a motorway to get to it," she whispered to Caroline. "I've seen this sort of thing on those holiday programmes."

The driver, still grinning, said nothing.

Club Maritimo was a vast complex, encompassing two small hotels with a dozen or so villas set in the hills behind them. The hotel terrace led down to a swimming-pool, two tennis-courts and a small bar, all surrounded by trees and flowers . . . and beyond was the sumptuous golden beach lined with palm-trees which edged the crystal-clear, turquoise Caribbean sea.

Jackie gasped at the splendour.

"I don't believe it!" said Caroline, her eyes filling with tears. "This is so . . . beautiful!"

They stood on the terrace, suitcases at their side, a cool breeze brushing their sweat-streaked faces, staring silently beyond the pool and out towards the open sea.

The coach driver, still grinning, sidled past them, carrying one of the elder passengers' luggage.

"Magnifico, eh?" he said.

"Magnifico," echoed Jackie and Caroline.

Their shared room was large, spotlessly clean and air-conditioned with an en-suite bathroom. The girls hurriedly unpacked, determined to swim in the pool before dinner was served in the hotel's restaurant.

"What d'you think we'll get?" asked Caroline as she hung her blouses, skirts and t-shirts in the spacious wardrobe.

"Dunno," replied Jackie, who bounced up and down on her bed, testing the mattress. "Beans on toast, probably."

Caroline turned and smiled at her. "D'you reckon?"

"Give over!" giggled Jackie. "Going by what we've seen so far, it'll be caviare!"

"Ugh!" they both screamed together, before bursting into laughter.

It took longer than they'd expected to unpack, finding a home for their clothes, their swimming costumes and the packet of tea-bags Caroline's mother had insisted she take with her. Then, realizing there was no time to swim before dinner, they showered, changed, put on their make-up and made their way to the restaurant.

The welcoming maitre d' led them to a white-clothed table in the corner of the room and handed them menus and the wine list.

Jackie grinned at her companion across the

small vase of bright yellow flowers set in the centre of the table.

"Posh, innit?" she said. Then, looking over Caroline's shoulder, she gave a faint squeal of delight.

"What's up?" asked Caroline.

She turned her head to follow Jackie's stare. Two men had entered the restaurant and were being greeted by the maitre d' as though they were long-lost friends. One was the burly minder from the aeroplane. The other was Duane Sheldon.

2

Jackie awoke in terror. During the night she'd been too excited to sleep and instead had lain on her bed listening to the delicious sound of the waves washing gently onto the nearby but, as yet, unexplored beach. She could hardly wait for sunrise so that she and Caroline could hurtle across the golden sands and plunge into the warm Caribbean. The steady shlep, shlep, shlep was soon topped, however, by the irritating, low hum of a mosquito, and remembering the particularly nasty bite she'd received in Tenerife, when her nose had taken on the appearance of a cricket ball, she'd pulled the thin, white sheet over her face for protection. Tucking the hem of it under the back of her head she at last fell into a deep sleep, exhausted from the day's travelling. And now, forgetting momentarily where she was, she'd opened her eyes to find herself encased like a mummy, her hair matted with sweat. She struggled to remove the tight shroud and sat bolt upright in bed, staring around the room. Then she remembered where she was.

Caroline's bed was empty and unmade. Jackie padded barefooted to the bathroom, calling her name.

"Caroline? Caroline?"

There was no response. The tiled floor was wet and a damp towel hung over the side of the bath. Cursing her friend for not waking her before going down to breakfast, Jackie hurried through the shower, roughly dried her red hair on a towel, slipped into a baggy, pale green t-shirt with shorts to clash, tied her well-worn and much-loved Reeboks and headed for the hotel's dining-room.

The last of the breakfasters was just leaving.

"I think they've finished serving, my dear," said an ancient, shuffling forward on his walking-frame.

Jackie passed among the tables, dodging the cheery waiters who were whisking away the breakfast condiments whilst resetting the room for lunch, and passed on through the huge patio doors to the pool. Here Caroline sat, in skimpy bikini, squinting through the bright sunlight at the twinkling water.

"Well, thanks very much!" said Jackie. She sat beside Caroline in one of the three cane chairs set round the small table.

"I wish I'd brought my sunglasses down with me," tutted Caroline. "I didn't think it'd be this sunny, so early in the morning."

Jackie looked at her watch. "It's half-past nine," she said. "Why didn't you wake me?"

"You were dead to the world," giggled Caroline. "Snoring your head off."

Jackie frowned, unsure. "I don't snore."

Caroline glanced sideways at her, grinning. "Really? You sure?"

"So, what was breakfast like?" asked Jackie. "I suppose you've been stuffing down eggs and bacon and pots of tea while I've been racing to get ready?"

"I didn't feel like anything," replied Caroline. "I sat at a table and nibbled at some toast, but that was only so I could get a good ogle at Duane Sheldon and his mates."

Jackie was disappointed. "I've missed them?"

"'Fraid so."

"Did they speak to you?"

"One of them winked at me. That fat one that I wouldn't touch with a barge-pole. You know, the one you fancied." She giggled.

"I didn't fancy any of them!" protested Jackie. "Except Duane Sheldon."

"Of course!"

"I don't suppose *he* winked at you?"

Caroline sighed. "I don't think he knows I exist. I don't think he knows what planet he's on, come to think of it. And he looked such a mess this morning."

This pleased Jackie. Looking as awful as most human beings do when their eyelids are still stuck together with sleep, would make the super-handsome pop star seem a wee bit more attainable. He always looked so perfect on the telly and in photos. And last night, watching him as he dug into his avocado vinaigrette, she'd been totally smitten.

"How *much* of a mess?" she asked eagerly.

"Well . . ." Caroline disappointed her, ". . . not *that* much of a mess. Not the sort of mess that you and me look over breakfast. But his hair was a bit . . . it was sort of . . ." she stopped and changed course. "What am I talking about?" she giggled. "He looked a real dish! I could've eaten him with my toast and marmalade."

Jackie screamed with laughter.

She stopped short when a good-looking man in white vest and Bermuda shorts arrived at her side with a tray.

"Sorry. I would've got three if I'd known," he said.

He placed two coffees onto the table. "Shall I get another one?"

'This is Glen," said Caroline. "He comes from Essex. Glen, this is my best friend Jackie."

"Hi!" smiled Glen. "Would you like a coffee? I'll go and get another one."

Jackie returned the smile. "Thanks. I'd love one."

The man left.

Jackie stared across at Caroline. "Well, it didn't take you long, did it?"

"We were only chatting," grinned Caroline. "He's nice though. I love all those black hairs popping out of the top of his vest. And those hairy legs."

"I expect you like the tattoo as well," grimaced Jackie.

"I love tattoos."

"They're vulgar," said Jackie. "My cousin's got one on his shoulder-blade. It's so common."

"Ooh, get you . . . just 'cause you're on a posh holiday," giggled Caroline.

"You don't *really* fancy him, do you?" asked Jackie.

"He's all right. He'll do for a laugh."

"But he's old," argued Jackie. "He's far too old for you."

"He's twenty-nine."

"Quite!"

They sat in silence until Glen returned and placed down the third coffee.

"Thanks, Glen," smiled Caroline. "Jackie was just saying how much she liked your tattoo."

Jackie glared at Caroline and blushed. She noticed the twinkle in Caroline's eyes and immediately saw the funny side of it.

"Oh, thanks," said Glen, seriously. "I've got one on my shoulder-blade too. A bird."

Jackie's eyes met Caroline's and both girls laughed.

"What'd I say?" asked Glen.

"Nothing, Glen," replied Caroline. "Don't worry. Jackie's got this thing about tattoos on shoulder-blades, you see. Isn't that right, Jackie?"

"D'you want to see it?" asked Glen, and without waiting for a reply he tore off his vest and turned his back on Jackie, showing off a blue swallow with a love-heart in its beak.

Jackie smirked. "It's lovely," she lied. "Really pretty."

Glen turned to face her, beaming contentedly at both girls. "Hey. I think we're all going to be good friends, don't you?"

"Yes, I do," Caroline beamed back. "It'll be great."

Jackie returned to the room and changed into her swimsuit, slipping a thin white blouse over the top. She packed her towel, sun oil and a not-yet-started paperback romance into her beach bag and descended to the hotel lobby.

The lift was full and the lobby had started to teem with scantily-dressed people carrying rolled-up towels and rafia mats and she wondered if the beach would look like those pictures she'd seen of Blackpool in August.

"Hi!" said the young man who approached her. She recognized him immediately as the lad from the plane — the one who'd asked about 'Blondie'.

"Pete. D'you remember?" He was still chewing. She wondered if it was the same piece of gum . . . stuck onto the side of his wash-basin last night perhaps and then scraped up for re-use this morning, once he'd cleaned his teeth.

"I remember," she replied softly.

"I'm with the film crew. Duane Sheldon's lot."

"Yes."

"They've left me behind to sort out a few things. Pity really 'cause I was hoping to go with them. They're shooting on Paradise Beach, a few miles up the road. I could've at least had my shirt off and got a tan while we worked. As it is, I've got to stay by the telephone, taking calls from London. Bore, eh?"

"Yes." She looked around the lobby for Caroline.

"We've taken a room here to use as an office. Third floor. What floor are *you* on?"

"First."

"Nice?"

"Very."

"Sea view?"

"No."

"Pity."

"It's nice."

"Of course, none of our lot stay here. We've got half a dozen villas up there in the hills. We can use the hotel facilities, but it gives us more freedom up there. We can have private little parties and that. Invite who we want back for the night." He smiled at her. "If you know what I mean."

She didn't return the smile. "I know what you mean."

"You going swimming, are you?" he asked, eyeing her up and down.

"Why else would I be dressed like this?" she replied civilly, thinking, what a bonehead this bloke was.

"The beach is really quiet," he said. "Most of the people who stay here spend all day by the pool, finger-clicking at the waiters. Yeah. It's a bit too quiet really over there. Not much about."

"I like it quiet," she said pointedly. "I can lie and read my book *in peace*."

* * *

19

The beach was everything Jackie had imagined: soft, clean sand fringed by palm-trees, and lapped gently by crystal-clear water. Through the heat-haze, it seemed to stretch for miles and miles. And as far as she could see, it was practically empty. At the most, there were a dozen people. She walked along the sea's edge, feeling the warm water running through her toes. Caroline and Glen paddled behind her, oblivious to the splendour surrounding them, lost in conversation about their respective home lives.

"I work in a bank," said Glen. "But I'm not just a clerk," he added quickly. "I'm a trainee manager. I should be getting my own branch any day now."

"You must earn a fair bit of money," said Caroline, wrapping her arm round his bare waist. "We couldn't have afforded a holiday like this if we hadn't won it in a competition."

"I sold my house," he volunteered. "I was married and she went off with another bloke. Some rich geezer from up West. Ugly an' all. She only went with him for his money. Anyway, I thought, why not just sell up? It was too big for me to rattle around in on my own. So I bought a little flat and invested the rest. And I thought I deserved a holiday. *She's* having one. So why not me? Three weeks in paradise. One down, two to go. Lovely!"

"Have you got any children?" asked Caroline.

"No. No time for kids. Been too busy earning a crust."

Jackie had stared ahead, trying to switch off the conversation behind her, but his thin, monotonous voice had cut right through the gentle sound of the warm Caribbean breeze shuffling through the palms.

"Jackie, haven't we gone far enough?" Caroline called. "Why don't we settle here?"

Jackie had no intention of spending the whole day lying beside these two, listening to their naff talk of money and houses and babies. The conversation, she was sure, was about to move onto cars. His BMW probably.

"You stay here," she replied. "I'm going to go down a bit further."

"Okay. If you like," said Caroline, sounding rather relieved that she wasn't going to be lumbered with her best friend as she chatted up Mr Tattoos.

"You sure you'll be all right on your own?" asked Glen.

"Sure."

She was delighted at the thought of being alone. She could think of nothing worse than spending the whole day with this banker.

He wrapped his strong, manly arms round her, pulling her closer to his chest, and as he planted a kiss on her sensuously parted lips he felt her heart beating in time with his. And he whispered "Oh, my darling. I love you so, so much . . ."

Jackie placed the novel face down in the sand, turned over on her back and allowed the sun to touch her well-protected face. Through the high-factor oil she'd used, she could just feel the warm rays gently stroke her cheeks. This was pure heaven. So peaceful.

She lay still for minutes, sinking into the sand, her body feeling as heavy as lead . . . her mind empty. In the distance she heard a giggle and hoped that Glen and Caroline hadn't decided to join her. She lifted herself onto one elbow and looked along the beach. They were a long way off; two little dots in the distance, lying flat on their bellies, wrapped round each other – not approaching. Thank goodness. And then she noticed a figure much closer to her, lying face down in the sand; slim, dark, sporting a pair of yellow swimming-trunks . . . he sat up, intending to turn over . . . handsome, smooth-skinned, tall . . . and he saw her looking at him. He smiled, shyly, flashing straight, white teeth before reaching into his bag and taking out a personal stereo. He untangled the wires, placed the tiny speakers into his ears and smiled again. She smiled back. Then he lay on his back, closed his eyes and appeared to sleep.

3

Jackie handed the room key to the receptionist and chased after the bobbing blonde head, disappearing down the steps towards the carpark.

"What's the rush?" she asked breathlessly, as she caught up with Caroline.

"I want to get away before Glen arrives."

Jackie was surprised. "But why? I thought you liked him."

"I do," said Caroline. "He's great. But I don't want to spend the rest of my holiday with him, do I?"

Both girls stood back and allowed a coach, carrying a group of pasty-skinned new arrivals, to manoeuvre its way along the narrow drive.

"I want to see if there are any other dishes on the beach."

"There weren't many there yesterday," said Jackie.

"Except Yellow Trunks."

Jackie grinned. "You leave Yellow Trunks alone. He's mine."

She scanned the car-park for the Land Rovers belonging to Duane Sheldon's party.

"D'you think they've left?" she asked disappointedly.

Caroline shrugged. "Who knows?"

"Morning!" yelled Pete as he leapt down the steps three at a time behind the girls.

Caroline smiled at Jackie. "Obviously not," she said.

"Well, the bonehead's still here, anyway," whispered Jackie.

"A long day today," said Pete, almost ignoring Jackie; his eyes fixed on Caroline. "They were off on location by sunrise."

The two girls walked on.

"Really?" replied Caroline coolly.

"We haven't been properly introduced yet have we?" drooled Pete.

"We haven't been introduced *at all* . . . but I know who you are," tutted Caroline, without stopping. "You're Pete . . . and I'm Blondie!"

"And here comes her boyfriend," giggled Jackie as she saw Glen's car turn into the drive.

"Oh well," said Caroline as she shrugged resignedly. "Looks as though Yellow Trunks is all yours today."

"Well, thanks for your generous offer," replied Jackie, bemused by Caroline's presumption that Yellow Trunks would prefer blondes.

"So, you're not going to ask me to join you two girls after all?" laughed Pete Bonehead in a good-humoured way.

"That's right," said Jackie as both girls headed for Glen's car.

Glen stepped out of his hired Jeep, just as a chauffeur-driven limousine swept past him and sped through the car-park towards the waiting Pete Bonehead. Pete blew a kiss through the rear window of the limo before opening its door and taking the hand of its occupant. A beautiful, tall, slim girl in the shortest of blue shorts and the tightest of t-shirts stepped out, kissed the fawning Pete on both cheeks and swished back her long, blonde hair with her fingertips before holding her pale, perfectly-structured face up to the sun.

"Who's she?" gasped Glen, his tattooed bicep flexing involuntarily.

"Some blonde bimbo, by the looks of it," Caroline hissed. She flicked back *her* hair with her fingertips, placed her arm into Glen's, turned him round and marched him towards the car-park exit.

"Hi, Jackie!" he said, turning his head to the redhead, following on behind, though his eyes stared straight across her shoulder at Bimbo and Bonehead, now climbing the steps, hand in hand towards the hotel lobby.

"Hi, Glen," replied Jackie, with a grin. "We weren't expecting you so early ... were we, Caroline?"

"I have a confession to make," he said, avoiding her gaze. "I wasn't in Paris. I spent the week in Amsterdam."

"I know," she replied, tears streaming down her cheeks. *"I knew all along. Janine told me. I just didn't want to believe it."* She began to sob. *"How could you do it, Brad?"*

A warm gust of wind suddenly buried the words in sand. Jackie picked up the book, tossed the sand into the air and having slipped in the piece of ragged paper she was using as a bookmark, she suspended the romance until she felt more . . . romantic. She left it beside her towel and strolled down to the water's edge, feeling the soles of her feet burning with every step.

For a while she wondered at the tiny silver fish, fearlessly swimming around her ankles, watching them forage in the sand which moved in small ridges before her toes, as the tide gently washed it to and fro. She stepped further in, feeling the warm water rise to her waist and then with a plunge, she swam underwater with the bigger fish, eyes opened wide, watching them as they watched her.

She surfaced and immediately felt the searing heat from the morning sun, burning into her gently-freckled face. And then she saw him. Yellow Trunks. The lean, brown body, running gazelle-like, way along the beach. As he strode past Caroline and Glen, Jackie saw the blonde head bob up and stare. Yellow Trunks was oblivious to Caroline's presence. He wasn't interested in blondes! Had he come to find his redhead?

Jackie felt her heart beating faster as the handsome figure came nearer and nearer, striding across the sand towards her towel and her dog-eared copy of *A Stranger Love*. He leapt the towel and ran on . . . and on . . . into the distance, not even glancing in her direction. She watched, her pounding heart now sinking rapidly, as he rounded the white rock at the far end of the beach and disappeared from view.

She sighed deeply and made her way slowly back towards the beach and her paperback, but as she reached the shallows to be greeted once again by the shoal of mini fish, she saw him reappear from behind the rock, not running now, but strolling. He walked towards the sea and dived in gracefully, skimming the surface dolphin-like before submerging for what seemed to be minutes at a time.

Jackie turned round again to face the horizon and paddled out, her eyes continuously scouring the gentle waves for the black, swept-back hair atop the exquisitely handsome face. He was nowhere to be seen. And suddenly there he was . . . closer this time. He disappeared again. And bobbed up, closer still. And this time he saw her. And he smiled. And her heart stopped! And she managed, though dead, to smile back at him.

She wondered if she should call out, "Hello!" or "Good Morning!" or "My name's Jackie. What's yours?" but she decided against it. Better to remain cool, slightly aloof. And anyway, with her nervous throat feeling as dry as sandpaper, she feared that any attempt to speak would just come out as a demented croak.

He was standing almost still now, treading

water, staring at her, flashing that oh, so beautiful smile. And then he lifted a hand and waved and called, "Hi!" And she was about to wave back when she noticed that his gaze had been directed towards the beach. She followed his stare and saw two figures, almost stamping her romance into the sand. It was Bonehead and Bimbo, waving frantically and calling, "Mason! Mason!"

Mason Yellow Trunks gave one last glance at Jackie, shrugged, smiled again and swam off towards the beach. She watched him longingly as he raced up the shore towards the waiting wavers ... she sighed despondently as he hugged and kissed Bimbo Blue Shorts ... and she grimaced ungraciously as she heard Bimbo Blue Shorts screech, "Mason! Darling!"

And as Mason Yellow Trunks and Bimbo Blue Shorts left the beach, arm in arm with Pete Bonehead, Jackie decided it was time to return to *A Stranger Love.*

Caroline was having her first holiday dip, leaving Glen snoring on the beach, when she saw Jackie swimming along the coast towards her.

"Don't tell me you're actually going to get wet!" yelled Jackie.

Caroline laughed. "Cor ... isn't this water warm?"

"Did you see Yellow Trunks?" asked Jackie as she swam closer to Caroline.

"Did you see who he went off with?"

"Yes!" grumbled Jackie. "That blonde bombshell! I don't stand a chance."

Caroline dipped her head under the sea and came up, squirting water from her mouth. "Ugh! It's so salty."

"D'you think they're together?"

"Probably," sighed Caroline. "But that doesn't mean we can't take him off her. All's fair in love and war, so my mum says. And anyway, she's not the only blonde bombshell around here."

"I don't want *you* getting anywhere near him," warned Jackie, only half-jokingly. "You've got Glen to contend with." She looked out across the beach. "And talking of the devil . . ."

Glen was hurtling down the beach towards them, his chunky frame thumping heavily on the sand.

"Geronimo!" he yelled.

"I'll see you later," said Jackie as she turned in the water and swam out to sea.

Glen dive-bombed just feet away from Caroline sending a huge wash across her and knocking her off her feet. Caroline screamed as she struggled to regain her footing, then shrieked with laughter as he repeated the action.

"Stop it!" she yelled.

Glen picked her up in his huge arms and lifted the screeching girl above his head.

"No, no, no . . . please, Glen," screamed Caroline.

Mercilessly, he threw her, spluttering, into the water.

She rose from the waves, laughing hysterically. "You pig!" she yelled.

Suddenly, she stopped when she heard a piercing

cry from Jackie, far out to sea – much further out than Jackie had intended on swimming.

"She's in trouble, Glen," said Caroline, in panic.

Glen immediately began to swim towards the screaming Jackie. He sped through the water, watched admiringly by Caroline; his huge frame, gliding through the waves like a torpedo.

Jackie continued to scream, even as Glen reached her. He grabbed hold of her and turned her on her back, dragging her effortlessly to shore and carrying her the last few metres, where he laid her gently on the sand.

"It's my leg!" cried Jackie.

Caroline raced to her side. "Cramp?"

"No. I've been stung. A jellyfish I think." She groaned. "Oh, it really hurts. It really, really hurts."

Insisting that she could return to the hotel without support, Jackie limped into the lobby. Her left calf hadn't swollen but had turned a deep shade of red. The receptionist saw her arrive and smirked knowingly as he hurried to her aid, helping her onto one of the three sofas set round the large yucca.

"Una medusa," he said. "Una . . . yellyfitch."

"Sí," replied Jackie. "A jellyfish. And it's very painful."

"Yes." He shook his head and looked appropriately glum.

"Is it dangerous?" asked Jackie. "Should I see a doctor?"

He smiled, sympathetically. "No. It happens all

the time. The pain will go in a few hours. I will get the waiter to bring you a drink, eh?"

"No, thanks," said Jackie. "I'll hobble up to my room and wash some of this sand off first."

The receptionist nodded politely and returned to the desk to fetch Jackie's key.

By lunchtime the pain had completely disappeared, though there was still a nasty red blotch where the creature had brushed her leg. Jackie felt good, her body tight and fit from swimming. Her freshly washed and lightly conditioned hair gleamed in the sunlight and the tan, linking her freckles, made her, she felt, look more attractive than she'd ever done. Dressed in shorts and t-shirt, she sat contentedly by the pool, sipping a long, cool, fresh orange juice, peering occasionally over the top of her sunglasses at some newly-weds frolicking in the water.

Caroline and Glen had promised to return before one o'clock to see how she was, and to have lunch with her. But as it reached almost two, Jackie decided to order a sandwich and eat alone. Then, realizing that she couldn't plan her whole holiday around Caroline's whims, she left the hotel by the side entrance, passed through the lane which divided the fields of sugar-cane and walked on, exploring the exotic countryside of Lacruz.

Apart from the odd flutter and squawk of a disturbed, brightly-coloured bird and the gentle rustle caused by the breeze drifting through the sugar-cane, the lane was deathly quiet. Obviously, tourists never touched this part of the island. They were happy to sit by the pool most days, occasionally wandering to the beach. And who could blame them for indulging in such luxurious surroundings? But Jackie wanted more. Lying on a sandy beach, engrossed in a paperback romance and listening to the waves lapping onto the shore was luxurious indeed, but, close your eyes for a few seconds and one could be on any beach in the world – in Tenerife, in Majorca or even, during one of those rare English summers, in Bournemouth.

The sugar-cane path began to widen, finally merging with a wide, dusty road leading three ways. Jackie took the left fork, carefully noting from which direction she'd come, knowing that if she got lost in this neck of the woods, she'd probably wander for hours without coming across another soul.

She heard the vehicle long before she saw the dust rising. And suddenly she was frightened. Perhaps this had been a foolish thing to do – to wander alone, without telling anyone where she was going. Who knows what the natives really felt about tourists invading their island? She couldn't be sure that everyone on Lacruz was as friendly as the waiters at the hotel.

The cloud of dust grew thicker as the car came nearer. A large car. A Land Rover. It skidded to a halt beside her and a good-looking grey-haired man in his forties yelled to her.

"Want a lift?"

An Englishman, definitely. A strong East London accent.

Jackie smiled appreciatively and was about to turn down the offer, when she saw the handsome blond in the passenger seat. He looked straight ahead, totally ignoring her.

Jackie gulped, nervously. "Well, I'm just walking really. Exploring."

"Then how about some lunch?"

She'd just had lunch. But she couldn't resist it. If she turned this down, Caroline would go mad. Come to think of it, Caroline would go mad anyway!

"Thanks. That would be really nice," she said.

The driver leapt out of the driving seat, helped Jackie up and then climbed back behind his steering-wheel. Then, cramped between this good-looking, if somewhat elderly driver and the un-smiling Duane Sheldon, Jackie was sped away into the distant villa-dotted hills.

"David Brinkley," he said. "Of course, you're far too young to know the name, but ask your mum if she's ever heard of me." He laughed.

Jackie toyed with the tuna salad in front of her. The villa patio's stunning view took in the sugar-cane fields, part of the beach and the whole of the Club Maritimo complex. Jackie wondered, if she stared long and hard at the hotel's pool, which appeared from this height to be as tiny as a child's paddling pool, whether she might just see Caroline and Glen searching for her. The idea amused her.

"Were you a pop star, then?" she asked.

"Photographer," he replied. "Still am, though I

have to admit that I did my best work in the Seventies."

"So, are you photographing Duane?" she asked, trying to take in the sullen pop singer who sat opposite her, silently draining a can of lager.

"Yeah. I'm trying to shoot some stills between the video takes. It's for the teeny-mags and, hopefully, if we get it right, the album cover."

And Duane spoke, for the first time. "He's good," he said. "Good photographer."

Jackie stared at him, hardly able to believe that he'd directed the words at her. Duane Sheldon, superstar, had actually spoken to her. He'd even looked at her. *Just!*

She immediately responded, hoping that this would be the beginning of a meaningful conversation. "How long are you here for, Duane?"

His portable phone rang. He whisked it off the table and answered it.

"Yeah . . . yeah . . . yeah. Not bad. You? Yeah . . ."

He looked across at the photographer. "I'll take it inside, David," he said. And without a nod or a wink to Jackie, he went into the villa, still talking into the phone.

"Yeah . . . yeah . . . yeah. If you like. Yeah . . . yeah . . ."

Jackie had finished her tuna salad and had passed a very pleasant thirty minutes in the company of the charming David Brinkley before he stated that he had to return to work. There were some background shots he wanted to line up, which didn't require Duane's presence, and he'd drop her off at her hotel on the way to the location.

"I'll organize a dinner or something," he said as he helped her into the Land Rover. "For you and your friend. What did you say her name was?"

"Caroline."

"I'll arrange a dinner for you and Caroline. I can't promise you that the star himself will be there, but you'll love the crew. Great set of blokes."

The Land Rover sped down the winding hills towards the Maritimo.

"I've met one of them," said Jackie. "Pete. He's always in the hotel."

"Oh, right," grinned David. "Did I say they were a great set of blokes? All except that one. He's a right pain in the butt."

Jackie laughed.

As they neared the main road which led to the hotel, Jackie recognized the limousine which was heading towards them.

David honked his horn as the two vehicles passed each other.

"Pity," said David. "They're going up to the villa and you've just missed them. That's Kristie, one of America's top models. She's going to be huge in Europe next year. She's doing the video with Duane. And I'm trying to persuade her agent to let me use her for the album cover."

Jackie looked back at the blonde, beautiful Bimbo Blue Shorts sitting in the back seat of the limo, with her arms wrapped around Yellow

Trunks ... whom she'd now quickly re-named Yellow T-Shirt!

"And who's the guy?" asked Jackie, trying to sound super-cool.

"That's my assistant," replied David. "Going to be a great, great photographer, mark my words. Mason. Smashing bloke. He's American. You'd love him."

I'm sure I would, thought Jackie.

She turned her head to look back at the limo, which was just negotiating the sharp bend ahead and as she did so, Mason Yellow T-Shirt, peering through the rear window, met her gaze and smiled.

4

Caroline rushed into the dining-room, almost knocking over the waiter who was on his way to deliver a pair of glassy-eyed kippers to an even-glassier-eyed pair of pensioners. She slumped breathlessly into the chair opposite Jackie and knocked back the glass of apple juice which her friend had ordered for her.

"I've just seen them leave," she gasped, excitedly. "The whole lot of them: Duane Sheldon, Bimbo Blue Shorts, Yellow Trunks . . . all of them."

Jackie was hardly awake, having slept so soundly drifting in dreams in which she was accompanied by Yellow Trunks and Duane Sheldon.

Duane was singing into a microphone placed on the beach while Jackie stood waist-deep in the sea, behind a tape-deck which was surrounded by speakers and other recording equipment. She was directing Duane's performance as she twiddled knobs and pulled levers. Then as a huge shark approached her, yelling "Geronimo!", Yellow Trunks plunged into the sea and rescued her from its jaws.

"I've ordered us some poached eggs," she mumbled. "Is that all right?"

Caroline tutted. "Did you hear what I said?"

"Yes. You've just seen them all leave."

"So. Why don't we join them? Why don't we go to Paradise Beach and watch them filming?"

Jackie was shocked. "You're joking, of course?"

"They won't mind," bubbled Caroline. "After all, you know them now, don't you? It's not as though we're just a couple of Duane Sheldon fans, is it? You had lunch with him yesterday. And he's invited us to dinner."

"I'm not just turning up at their location!" said Jackie firmly. "That's really pushing ourselves onto them. I couldn't do it!"

Caroline began to sulk.

"Oh, come on," said Jackie. "We can't. Let's just wait until we get an invitation, Caroline."

"You can be such a stick-in-the-mud some-times," hissed Caroline.

The waiter arrived with the poached eggs and as soon as he'd left, Caroline pushed hers aside.

"I'm not hungry," she said. "I'm going back to the room to put my sun cream on. I'll see you later." And she swept out of the dining-room.

Jackie's appetite had suddenly diminished, but to save embarrassment, she ate her poached egg . . . and half of Caroline's.

By the time Jackie had returned to the room to

change into her swimming costume, Caroline had left. Suspecting that she'd gone to the beach without her, Jackie first checked the bar, the pool area and even the car-park. There was no sign of her. She found Glen waiting at reception, looking very despondent. His face lit up when he saw her.

"The receptionist told me you'd gone," he said. "I couldn't believe you'd just leave without me."

He sounded, thought Jackie, rather pathetic and she knew that if he continued to react in this way every time Caroline sloped off somewhere, she'd soon give him the elbow. Caroline couldn't stand wet men, even though with her dominating personality, these were often the types of men she attracted.

"*I* didn't leave without you, Glen," she explained, kindly, "but Caroline was in a bit of a sulk and she's just disappeared."

"When?" asked Glen, in a panic. "Last night?"

"No." Jackie took Glen's chunky hand in hers. "This morning. After breakfast. She's probably gone straight to the beach. Let's go and look for her."

"Did you have a row or something?" asked Glen as they reached the beach, scanned the half-dozen or so people there, and noted that Caroline wasn't among them.

"A little disagreement," replied Jackie. "Don't worry. You don't know Caroline like I do. She's very headstrong."

"But where would she have gone?" he murmured dejectedly.

Jackie shrugged.

"I think we should wait here for her," he suggested. "She'll come, I'm sure." He sat on the beach, staring mournfully out to sea.

Jackie smiled at his optimism, set her towel down on the sand, lay on her front and buried herself in *A Stranger Love*.

She heard his footsteps in the hall and, with trembling heart, she stood before the spluttering log-fire waiting for him to enter. She wondered how he'd react when he saw her. Would he still feel the same? It was almost too much to bear.

"She's not coming, is she?" said Glen at last. He looked at his watch. "It's nearly one o'clock."

Jackie closed her book and stood, shaking out her sandy towel.

"Let's go back to the hotel," she said sympathetically. "You're obviously not going to settle until you find her."

"Paradise Beach?" questioned the receptionist. "Aah, sí. La Playa Paraíso. Today, everyone wants to go to La Playa Paraíso."

"I'm sure they do," said Jackie, her suspicion confirmed.

"It's not far, but too far to walk," continued the receptionist. "You could hire a bike from Señor Moreno. He runs the Bar Copa below the Maritimo Gymnasium."

"We don't need a bike, thanks," interrupted Glen. "I've got a car."

The receptionist grinned. "Then it's easy. Take the lower road towards San Cristobal and follow the signs for Los Molinos. It's easy."

"Thanks," said Jackie.

She turned to Glen. "So, let's go, amigo!"

It wasn't as easy as the receptionist said it would be. Finding San Cristobal, a tiny village of two dozen or so white houses with a church which appeared to be far too big for the amount of inhabitants who lived there, was no problem. But the road to Los Molinos split several times without any road signs to direct them. And as Glen squeezed his Jeep along several narrow lanes between groves of lemon and guava trees, they both began to feel that they'd taken the wrong fork; that this pot-holed road led nowhere.

"Don't you think we'd better turn back?" suggested Jackie. "This can't be right."

Glen laughed. "And how am I supposed to turn the car round?"

"Couldn't you reverse?" asked Jackie. "Honestly, Glen, if we go much further I think we'll end up in some farmer's field."

Glen put the Jeep into reverse and peered back over his shoulder as he recovered his tracks. The vehicle bumped up and down, throwing both its occupants backwards and forwards as its wheels found each pot-hole.

"Careful!" shrieked Jackie. "The last thing we need now is a puncture."

"Don't worry," replied Glen, comfortingly. "These jeeps can stand anything."

There was a terrific bang and Glen wished he hadn't spoken so soon.

Jackie sighed. "Famous last words?"

"Famous last words!" agreed Glen. "Let's hope the spare tyre's OK." And he leapt down and started searching for the jack.

An hour had passed before Glen had managed to remove the wheel.

"Why do they have to put them on so tight!" he grumbled.

Both he and Jackie were dripping with sweat, covered in dust, and extremely thirsty.

"For all those muscles, you're not exactly strong are you?" Jackie giggled. "I could have got that wheel off in half the time." She attempted to flex her almost non-existent biceps.

Glen's face grew thunderous. "Oh, really?" he snapped. "Here!" He handed her the wheel spanner. "You put the spare on! Call me when it's done!"

He stormed off and sat at the side of the road, breathing heavily as he wiped a pool of sweat from his forehead.

Jackie approached him. "I was only joking," she said. "Sorry. I don't know how to do it. I was only trying to cheer you up."

He glared up at her. "I work in a bank!" he said. "I'm not a car mechanic! I hate cars. That's why I hired something reliable. So I wouldn't have this problem."

"Sorry," she repeated.

"Just because I've got a beautiful body," he added, "it doesn't mean that I can fix cars!"

She was about to walk away from him, hardly able to believe such arrogance. Then she noticed he was grinning.

"Despite the biceps and the tattoos, I'm a pen-pusher," he said with a smile. "I'm not tough. I never said I was."

She smiled back and flopped beside him on the dusty road.

"I'm so thirsty," she said. "I'd give anything for a glass of water."

"Me too." He looked up at the branches above them, covered with bright yellow fruit. "How d'you feel about sucking on a lemon?"

She looked up too, saw the fruit and felt her mouth begin to water. "I'd cringe at the idea," she said, "in normal circumstances. But . . . oh, yes please! I'd love a lemon."

They both laughed.

He stood and stretched, tearing two of the largest lemons from their branch and handing one to Jackie.

She ripped away the peel with her teeth and sucked on the sour fruit, her eyes watering and her mouth going into an involuntary spasm as the juice hit the back of her throat.

"Good, isn't it?" spluttered Glen. The insides of his cheeks recoiled from the acidity as his tongue did a backward flip. "It's really, really . . ."

"Foul!" said Jackie.

"Foul!" agreed Glen.

Jackie suddenly shrieked with laughter.

"What am I doing?" she gasped. "I'm miles from anywhere, with a bloke I don't know, sitting on a dusty road, sucking a lemon!"

The ridiculous situation also struck him as being very funny. They both laughed, the laughter growing and growing until they were convulsed like two crazed hyenas.

Finally they managed to control themselves and looked at each other. They were both red in the face, still running with sweat, still thirsty and both feeling panicky about the jacked-up Jeep with only three wheels.

"Come on," said Jackie. "I'll help you. It can't be that difficult."

It *wasn't* that difficult. And within half an hour the Jeep was reversing once again across the pot-holes.

They reached a clearing, turned the vehicle around and set off again towards what they hoped would be Los Molinos.

"Why would she want to go to Paradise Beach without us?" asked Glen. "I know she's interested in the filming and all that, but if we'd all gone together it would've been a laugh, wouldn't it?"

Jackie shrugged. "We're not sure she has gone there, are we? And even if that's where she set out for, it doesn't mean she found it. Look at us! I just hope she's not stuck down some country lane miles from anywhere, sucking lemons!"

He began to sound serious. "I really like her, Jackie. There was something about her, the minute I started speaking to her."

"You don't know her properly, Glen," Jackie tried to warn him. "She's great, but don't get too involved with her. It might spoil your holiday. Caroline's very independent. She could easily hurt you."

"I'm too old to get hurt," he replied. "Hardened to life after what *she* did to me."

"Your wife?"

He didn't reply; he seemed lost in thought.

"I'm not saying you shouldn't have a good time with Caroline. It's just . . ."

She stopped.

"Sorry, Glen," she continued. "It's got nothing to do with me. It just sounds like sour grapes, doesn't it?"

He grinned. "More like sour lemons."

They both laughed.

"Look!" Jackie suddenly yelled.

Ahead of them they noticed that the road, which was gradually widening, was leading to the foot of a hill, on top of which were three white windmills. A sun-bleached and very welcome signpost pointed them the way to Los Molinos.

They returned to the hotel two hours later, parked up, rushed to the poolside and ordered a jug of ice-cold water and an orange juice each.

"I don't think I've ever been so thirsty in my life," gasped Jackie as she quickly downed the water.

"Me neither," agreed Glen.

The search for Caroline had been fruitless . . . and Paradise Beach hadn't quite come up to their expectations; the hotel's beach appearing far more attractive. However, it *was* miles from anywhere and so it was understandable as to why the film crew had chosen the location. They certainly wouldn't be disturbed by curious tourists ruining the long-shots by getting into frame and waving at the camera.

By the time Glen and Jackie had arrived, Duane Sheldon and gang had left, leaving only the tyre-marks of their Land Rovers in the sand. They were still unsure as to whether Caroline had managed to trace them. And as far as Jackie was concerned, it was unimportant. What *was* of importance, was to get a drink. Quickly. Before she and Glen collapsed from dehydration.

Jackie saw the Land Rover appear in the hotel drive and was grateful that Glen had chosen that very moment to go to the loo. She wouldn't have wanted to watch Glen's face as Caroline climbed out of the vehicle with Duane Sheldon hot on her heels. She'd have hated to see Glen's reaction as Duane hoisted Caroline's hired pushbike from the back seat. And it would have been almost unbearable to watch Glen . . . watching Duane . . . holding Caroline . . . as he kissed her . . . before leaping back into his Land Rover and speeding away.

5

Neither Jackie nor Caroline were disappointed to see the rain. They were as brown as berries and both had been saying earlier how they could do with a day's rest from the constant heat. Besides, it would give them the opportunity to explore Santiago, Lacruz's main town. They sat in the hotel lobby with many of the other guests, all waiting for the early-morning bus which left daily for the town centre.

"He was really nice," said Caroline, sipping a can of Coke and staring out through the glass doors at the rain, now beating at the heads of the hibiscus. "He wasn't a bit like I thought he would be."

"I know," replied Jackie flatly. "I've met him."

She'd had no opportunity yesterday to tell Caroline what she'd thought of her behaviour. As soon as Duane Sheldon had left, Glen had returned from the loo and, delighted to see the safe return of his holiday romance, had listened enthusiastically to Caroline's description of how she'd gone for a bike ride and had got lost. There was no mention of Paradise Beach, nor the video shoot. And Glen didn't ask any questions. Maybe he didn't want to know.

The three of them had had supper together in the hotel restaurant then had crossed to Bar Copa for a few drinks before Jackie had decided it was time for bed, leaving the two love-birds together. She'd stayed awake until one o'clock waiting for Caroline to return, intent on giving her a piece of her mind. But sleep overtook her and when she woke, during the early hours, and saw the blonde head in the bed on the far side of the room, she decided to let it rest. What Caroline did from now on, Jackie determined, wouldn't affect her in any way. As far as she was concerned, Caroline could do just as she pleased. Just so long as she kept her hands off Mason Yellow Trunks.

"Is Glen coming to town with us?" she asked.

Caroline smiled. "I thought about ringing him at his hotel, but he'll know where we are, won't he? We're obviously not going to the beach on a day like today."

With brakes squealing, the rickety single-decker pulled up in front of the hotel and the holiday-makers immediately tumbled down the steps, umbrellas aloft, scrambling for window seats.

Santiago was an odd mixture of large colonial houses, shanties and modern office blocks. The town's centre, La Plaza, was a huge market-place from which there led several narrow lanes lined with grand shops, easily equalling those found in London's Bond Street. Jackie and Caroline, dodging the showers, wandered the market-stalls, fingering the elegantly-carved mahogany figurines, trying on the straw hats and sandals and noting the low prices of the jewellery and perfumes — perfect presents to take home to their mums.

"There's Glen!" said Jackie, suddenly.

Caroline grabbed her arm. "Where?"

Jackie pointed across to the fish stall where Glen, jacket collar turned up against the rain, was watching a large, blueish crab gasping its last breath.

"There."

"Come on," said Caroline as she led Jackie through the market away from Glen, towards a bar-café where an awning protected huddled shoppers from another downpour. "He's probably searching for me," she added. "I'm not really in the mood for him this morning."

Jackie said nothing.

"Fancy a drink?" asked Caroline as she peered into the café and saw a group of caucasian boys, early twenties, sipping pints of lager.

"If you like," replied Jackie innocently.

The four lads watched as the girls approached the bar, and drooled over Caroline as Jackie ordered two Cokes. As they picked up their drinks and headed for a small table, the plainest of the boys stepped forward and introduced himself.

"Rupert," he announced, slurring his upper-class English accent. "We're from London."

"Oh, yeah?" said Caroline.

The fair-haired boy sat at the table in the only other vacant seat. His friends turned back to the bar, talking among themselves, allowing Rupert to continue with his chat-up lines.

"So, where are you from?" he asked both girls, though his eyes were focused on Caroline.

Jackie didn't like the boy. He was, she was sure, drunk. And it was still only eleven a.m.

"We live here," she lied, sounding even more upmarket than the drunken Rupert. "Our father owns the Maritimo Complex. Do you know it?"

The boy's mouth dropped open. "Really?"

Caroline's mouth dropped open too. She stared at Jackie, her eyes twinkling.

"Yes," went on Jackie. "We're sisters." She put out her hand to shake Rupert's. "I'm Madeleine and this is Daisybell."

Caroline's eyes widened as she stared at Jackie in disbelief, mouthing in horror, *"Daisybell?"*

She wondered why Jackie had chosen such an extraordinary name for her. Daisybell? Why Daisybell? The corners of her mouth twitched and she knew she wouldn't be able to keep this up.

"We were born here, actually," said Jackie. "We've never been to London, have we, Daisybell?"

Caroline grinned. "No," she replied. "Madeleine and I have always wanted to go to London. We hear it's very nice. Don't we, Madeleine?"

Jackie knew she was about to burst. "Yes, Daisybell. We hear Knightsbridge is rather special." She managed to keep her laughter in check, staring wide-eyed at the bemused Rupert.

"So, what do you do for a living?" asked Rupert, quickly informing them whilst trying to impress them with the line, "We're all stockbrokers."

"What do we do for a *what?*" giggled Jackie, her vowels becoming ludicrously elongated, sounding like Princess Margaret.

Caroline picked up on the joke. "We don't do anything," she grinned. "We're rich!"

"Daisybell and I will inherit most of Lacruz one day," added Jackie. "Won't we, Daisybell?"

Rupert's face suddenly changed. His eyes became cold as he smirked at them. "Really?" he said. "You must think I'm stupid!"

He stood and walked back to join his friends at the bar.

Jackie looked at Caroline. "He must've known all along," she said.

"I'm not surprised," screeched Caroline. "Daisybell? Where did you get a name like that?"

Both girls crumpled over their Cokes, hooting with laughter.

"You gonna let me in on the joke?" said a voice.

Jackie looked up to see the photographer, David Brinkley, towering above them.

"Oh! Hello," stammered Jackie. "What are you doing here?"

"Can't shoot anything today, can we?" replied David. "Not in this weather. So we thought we'd take a look at Santiago."

We? thought Jackie. She looked around and saw that the disgruntled Rupert and his stockbroker pals were just leaving without glancing back.

Their place at the bar was being taken by the whole Duane Sheldon gang, including the star himself. Her eyes settled on Mason Yellow Trunks who, with his arm wrapped around Bimbo Blue Shorts, looked across at her and smiled.

"This is Caroline, by the way," said Jackie quickly. "Caroline, this is David. He's a photographer."

"We've already met," replied David. "Caroline came up to the house with Duane yesterday. For lunch."

"Did she?" said Jackie.

Caroline looked at Jackie, feigning innocence. "I thought I told you."

"Drinks, girls?" interrupted David. "What can I get you?"

Caroline was displeased that Jackie had hustled her out of the bar before she'd managed to make a firm date with Duane Sheldon.

"I don't want to spend all day stuck in a bar," snapped Jackie. "I want to see some more of the town. The bus goes back at three o'clock."

"If you'd left me to do the chatting," argued Caroline, "I could've persuaded them to run us back to the hotel in the Land Rovers."

Jackie passed on through the fruit and vegetable stalls, piled high with plantains and okra and coconuts. Caroline followed at her heels.

"It was best to leave," she said. "You don't want to appear too eager. These pop stars are used to fans throwing themselves at their feet."

"But I *am* eager!" Caroline's voice began to

rise. "And I'm not a fan! I don't even like his music. I just like *him*!"

"And fancy asking them all to the beach barbecue tonight!" tutted Jackie. "It's a private do, you know. It's for the hotel guests."

"And their *friends*!" quoted Caroline from the invitations they'd been handed earlier by the desk-clerk. "Anyway, you won't complain if Yellow Trunks turns up, will you?"

"I will if he turns up with Bimbo Blue Shorts," replied Jackie. "That'll be great fun for me, won't it?"

"Caroline! Jackie!" called Glen, as he hurtled through the market towards them.

"Oh, no," Caroline said under her breath.

Jackie called out happily to him. "Hiya, Glen. We thought we'd see you here." She turned to Caroline. "Be nice to him!" she hissed. "He hasn't done you any harm. Don't hurt him, Caroline. He doesn't deserve it."

Glen rounded a stall loaded with bejewelled conches and approached them.

"Don't mention the barbecue!" said Caroline, panic tightening her voice. "If they both turn up together, I don't know what I'll do!"

Glen reached them, puffing slightly. He put his arms round Caroline's neck and kissed her.

"I went to the hotel," he said, "but they told me you'd come into town on the bus."

"Not a beach day, is it?" smiled Caroline.

"I can take you back in the jeep, if you like," he suggested. "You and Jackie, of course."

"Thanks, Glen," said Caroline. "But I want to

get the bus. It's part of the holiday experience, isn't it? Doing it as the natives do it."

Jackie looked at her with raised eyebrows. What a line!

"So, what are we doing tonight, then?" asked Glen.

Jackie wondered how Caroline was going to get out of this one.

"Oh, Glen!" she gasped. "Didn't I tell you? There's a beach barbecue, set up by the hotel. But it's only for guests. Sorry."

Glen looked glum. "Oh!"

"Sorry!"

"So that means I can't see you then?"

"I'll see you tomorrow," Caroline said brightly. "But not tonight, Glen. You don't mind, do you?"

The Maritimo had excelled itself in presenting a first-class barbecue constructed on part of the beach near to the hotel. Usually quiet, tonight the place was jumping. Jackie hoped that this wouldn't encourage more of the hotel's guests to start using the beach, rather than the pool, during the daytime. She'd got accustomed to lying alone and losing herself in *A Stranger Love*, without being bothered by hordes of holiday-makers.

The sun was just beginning to set, turning the sky almost scarlet; a perfect backdrop for the quarter-moon, already visible. The smell of Creole cooking filled the air: mullet, sardines and shellfish. To the accompaniment of a four-piece steel band Jackie helped herself to pumpkin soup and prawns served with cassava and bread fruit, following this with a mixture of mango and paw paw. Everything was washed down with a fruit-filled and very strong rum punch.

"What a life!" sighed Caroline as she nibbled on a piece of fresh coconut. "All I need now, to make this a perfect evening, is for Duane to turn up."

"He won't," said Jackie.

She was wrong.

He arrived ten minutes later.

And he was accompanied by David Brinkley, Mason Yellow Trunks . . . and Bimbo Blue Shorts!

"I knew it!" said Jackie. "*You'll* be all right. But my one's brought his girlfriend with him."

Having greeted the girls and helped themselves to the Maritimo's splendid fare, Duane Sheldon led Caroline away from the group where they sat under a palm, whispering sweet nothings. Jackie watched enviously as the pop star wrapped his arms round his latest conquest and kissed her. David and Mason were engrossed in conversation with Bimbo Blue Shorts, who tonight could have been re-christened Bimbo - White - See - Through - Blouse - Tied - Up - To - Reveal - Plenty - Of - Tanned - Navel.

Carrying a second glass of rum punch, Jackie wandered far away from the crowd, making her way along the beach, watching the huge, red sun finally disappearing behind the horizon. Suddenly the sky was filled with stars, the cicadas ceased their constant high-pitched scratching and, from where she stood, the lapping of the water began to top the distant sound of the steel band and the animated chatter of the revellers.

She sat on the sand a few metres away from the water's edge, watching the reflection of the tiny crescent moon and dreading the arrival of the day when she'd have to return to London, leaving this piece of paradise behind her. Her mind wandered back to school, her mum and dad . . . and her new job.

"Hi!"

The voice made her jump.

Jackie looked up to see Mason Yellow Trunks's handsome face smiling down on her. She almost stopped breathing. She gulped and managed to croak back, "Hi."

"May I join you?" he asked. The accent was American. West Coast, from what Jackie could remember through *L.A. Law* via *Beverly Hills, 90210*.

"Of course," she replied.

He sat on the sand beside her, his denimed legs stretched out towards the sea, the sleeves of his thin, yellow shirt flapping in the gentle breeze.

"Mason," he said.

"Jackie."

He smiled, his straight, white teeth gleaming through the perfectly structured, tanned lips.

"Hi, Jackie."

She smiled back. "Hi, Mason."

"I've been watching you," he said. "It's great to talk to you at last."

"You're American," she said and then inwardly cursed herself for making such a crass remark.

"Sure am!" he laughed. "San Francisco. You ever been?"

"No. But I'd like to."

"Shall we go *now*?"

She smiled at him. "All right."

He took her hand, stood and pulled her to her feet, leading her closer to the sea.

"What are you doing?" she asked.

"Let's swim . . . to America," he grinned.

"You're daft," she said, grinning back.

She sat again and he joined her, turning on his side to face her, leaning up on one elbow, staring at her.

"So . . . you're on holiday."

"And you're working. I know all about you," she said. "David told me. You're a photographer."

"You know all about me, do you?" He laughed loudly. "So you know that my name is Mason Wright . . . that I'm nineteen years old . . . that I was born in Los Angeles . . . that my father is a film director (employed) and my mother is an actress (unemployed) . . . that I've been working in Chelsea as a photographer assisting David Brinkley and that I've just been offered a top photographic job back in L.A. which I intend to accept. You also know of course that I'm a Scorpio, interested in rock music and that I'm married with two small children."

The last statement upset her. She stared at him, trying hard not to show her disappointment, replying softly, "Well, thanks for telling me your life story."

"And it's all true," he said. "Apart from the

married with two children bit. I'm single and very available."

He placed his hand on hers.

"But what about Bimb—?" She stopped. "What about that blonde model girl. Aren't you dating her?"

"Kristie?" he smiled. "No. No way. Not my type."

Jackie sighed . . . and then hoped that it hadn't been audible. She didn't want to appear too keen.

6

"You are silly, you know," said Caroline.

Jackie brushed the sand from the print and turned the page. Her friend's presence, so close, intruding on *A Stranger Love* was an irritation. It was the first time since they'd arrived in paradise that Caroline had lain beside her while sunbathing, bombarding her with mindless chatter.

"You should've accepted his offer," she went on. "I mean, you really like him. And he likes you. So why did you refuse to go back with him?" She sighed and turned over on her back. "I don't understand you sometimes, Jackie. I really don't."

Over breakfast Caroline had jabbered on and on about Duane Sheldon.

"He's so attentive," she said, having already outlined the story of the chat-up. "He makes you feel as though you're the most important person in the world."

Jackie took another piece of toast and spread it thickly with apricot jam.

"I think he's fallen for me," added Caroline. "And it wouldn't take much for me to fall in love with him, I can tell you."

"Don't be ridiculous," mumbled Jackie through the toast. "You don't even know him. He probably treats all of his pick-ups like that."

Caroline flared. "I'm not a pick-up! He really likes me. And I like him. We've got a lot to talk about."

"I bet he didn't ask anything about you," tutted Jackie. "I bet he doesn't even know where you live."

Caroline stood. "I'm going to get my swimming things," she said. "I'll see you in the lobby."

Jackie watched her go, ashamed that she'd reacted so badly to Caroline's enthusiastic chatter. Such a reaction, she was sure, would only be interpreted as envy. She knew she should have oohed and aahed in the appropriate places, encouraging what appeared to Caroline to be a blossoming romance. But Jackie felt sure that her friend was just being used. She'd been a young pop star's one-night stand and as sure as God made little apples, Caroline was going to get hurt.

She sipped back the last of her coffee, placed her napkin on the crumb-sprinkled tablecloth and left the dining-room. She'd intended to go up to the room and to make her apologies after which, they'd both hug each other, have a good giggle . . . and then everything would be all right. She stopped when she saw Caroline standing in the lobby, talking to a glum-faced Glen.

"Look ... you don't own me you know," she said. "It's all been very nice. But that's it. I'm sorry."

He looked as though he were about to burst into tears.

"But what have I done wrong?" he asked.

She sighed. "You haven't done anything wrong, Glen. But I'm dating someone else now. I'm really sorry." She gave him a sympathetic smile, turned her back on him and headed for the staircase.

"Caroline!" he called desperately.

She leapt the steps two at a time, without looking back.

Jackie approached him.

"Glen? What's up?"

He could hardly speak. "She's dumped me. She said she's got someone else."

"Oh," replied Jackie. "I'm sorry."

"Has she?" he asked pathetically. "When did all this happen?"

Jackie shrugged. "Last night, I think."

"At that barbecue?"

"Yes."

"Who is it? Someone from the hotel?"

Jackie hung her head, too embarrassed to go into the details.

"It's not that boring bloke who works for Duane Sheldon, is it?"

"No," Jackie half-whispered. "It's not Pete."

"Then who?"

"I don't know, Glen," she lied. "But, look ..." She took his hand, gently, "... you know what holiday romances are all about. They can never be more than just a bit of fun. A few days of romping in the sand . . . and then . . ."

"It was more than that to me," he said. "I really like her, Jackie. I don't want to lose her."

"I'm sorry, Glen," sighed Jackie. "But what can I say?"

She began to break away from him. She could see that if she lingered longer there'd be tears . . . and she knew she couldn't cope with that. Not so soon after breakfast!

"Couldn't I come to the beach with you?" he asked. "Maybe I could persuade her . . ."

"I don't think that's a very good idea, Glen," she replied kindly. And then, simply to give him an iota of hope, she added, "Why don't you come to see her this evening? Who knows? Maybe she'll have changed her mind."

"I mean," said Caroline. "It could've turned into something really special! All you had to do was to come back to the villa with us. We could've had a few drinks and that. I'm sure if you'd said that you wanted to go back to the hotel, Mason would've taken you. Just by going with him to the villa . . . well, you wouldn't have been agreeing to anything else would you?"

Jackie closed her book and pushed it aside.

"I'm going for a swim," she said.

She floated on her back in the water, wondering how she'd explain to Caroline that tonight she wanted to be alone.

After the despairing Glen had left the hotel, the desk-clerk had called to Jackie, informing her that there was a phone call from a Mr Wright.

She took the receiver in her trembling hand.

"Jackie?"

"Hi, Mason," she gulped.

"What are you doing tonight?" he asked. "Are you free?"

"Caroline and I haven't really discussed anything yet," she replied. "Why?"

"I thought you might like to go to Fantasma," he said. "It's a huge disco in Santiago."

"We'd love to," she replied excitedly.

"No. Not *we*!" he said coolly. "I'm not asking Caroline too. I'm not into threesomes." He laughed. "Just you. You and me. How's about it?"

"*I'd* love to," she said.

"It's a late start," he explained. "So if I pick you up about ten?"

"Fine!" she said.

She paddled up to the beach and lay on her towel, drying off in the sun. How would she tell Caroline that she had a date tonight? That she and Mason were going to a disco . . . alone!

Caroline turned over onto her front again.

"I mean, when you think about it, you were really stupid, Jackie," she said. "You've been lusting after Mason Yellow Trunks since we got here. And as soon as he asks you up to his villa, you go all prudish and turn him down. You're really stupid."

"Why don't you just mind your own business!" snapped Jackie suddenly.

Caroline was shocked. She sat bolt upright and stared at her friend.

"Ooh, I'm sorry I spoke, I'm sure!" she said.

"You keep calling me stupid, Caroline. You keep trying to push your own sub-standards onto me. And I'm not having it! I've got my own code of behaviour, thank you, and I don't need to be told by someone like you how to conduct myself."

Caroline was furious. "What do you mean, someone like me? What's that supposed to mean?"

"You've got Glen breaking his heart over you," she said, "while you're throwing yourself at some pop star who's out for all he can get! So don't start telling me how to behave, Caroline!"

Caroline's face crumpled and Jackie immediately wished her comments hadn't been quite so vitriolic.

"I'm sorry," she said. "Don't cry, Caroline. I didn't mean that. Honest."

Caroline began to snivel. "It's only because I wish you had a date, that's all," she said. "I hate to think of you being on your own while I'm having fun. I know how desperate you are to get a boyfriend."

Jackie began to boil again. "I'm not desperate, thank you very much. You make me sound as though, at the grand old age of sixteen, I've been left on the shelf — that no one wants me!"

"I didn't mean that." Caroline wiped the tears on the back of her hand. "It's just that . . ."

"As a matter of fact," added Jackie. "I've got a date tonight. Mason's taking me to a disco!"

Caroline's mouth dropped open. She stared at her friend for a few seconds. Then she lay back on her towel, closed her eyes and pretended to sleep.

Mason arrived dead on ten o'clock and was met by Jackie, rushing across the car park to greet him.

"I took a taxi," he said. "The Land Rovers are in demand this evening."

"There's a problem, I'm afraid," explained Jackie.

"Caroline?"

"I couldn't leave her behind, Mason. D'you mind if she comes with us? She promises she won't hang around all night."

He shrugged. "Not a lot I can do about it, if you've already asked her, is there?"

Caroline descended the steps, dressed in white, hoping that there'd be U.V. lighting at the disco, thus making her stand out like a beacon in the night.

"Are you annoyed?" asked Jackie.

He grinned. "Nope. Though *she* might be, when she sees who's there . . . with another date."

Fantasma was on two floors, the lower floor consisting of an enormous dance area, two bars, a mini restaurant, a pool table and several cloakrooms. The upper floor was quieter; silent pop videos being flashed simultaneously on the twenty or so giant screens.

Mason found an intimate table for two and

dragged up a third chair for Caroline, hoping it was only for temporary use.

"I won't hang about," said Caroline. "I just hope someone'll ask me to dance soon."

A waiter arrived.

"I'll get these," said Caroline, surprised that Mason didn't try to stop her.

"I'll have a beer," he drawled.

"A beer and two Cokes," ordered Caroline, assuming that Jackie would stick to her usual drink.

"I don't suppose the others are coming, are they?" she asked Mason. "Or are they all working tonight?"

"I'm not sure about David," replied Mason, teasing the girl. "He said he might come."

"And?"

"And?" Mason laughed.

"And what about the others. You know!"

"Oh, I see," said Mason. "By the others, you mean the star of the show? Our Duane?"

"Well? Is he coming?" asked Caroline.

Mason nodded across the bar, indicating that Duane Sheldon had already arrived.

Caroline followed his gaze and saw the pop star leaning on the trellised door leading to the veranda.

"See you," she said.

She leapt from her seat and rushed across to her new lover, flinging her arms round his neck.

"Oh, dear," grimaced Mason. "How embarrassing."

Duane unwound the girl's arms and took a step sideways, kissing her on the cheek.

"Hello, darling," he said.

His eyes were cold, his mouth unsmiling.

"Aren't you pleased to see me?" she asked.

"No. Not tonight," he replied. He walked away from her towards a stunning black girl in a tight, red leather skirt, who was making her way from the ladies.

Caroline stared as the man she felt she'd conquered kissed the girl, wrapped his arm around her thin waist and propelled her towards the staircase which led down to the dance floor.

"Oh, no," gasped Jackie.

"That's how the cookie crumbles," grinned Mason. "I knew it would end in tears."

It was either Billy Druid's Blue on Blue, with its soulful sax, or it was the way in which Mason held her tightly in his arms which had made the hairs on the back of Jackie's head stand to attention. Maybe it was a combination of both. They'd danced until their faces glistened with sweat, but now, smooching around to this beautiful ballad, Jackie felt really ... alive. She ran her fingernails across the back of his wet, pale blue shirt and felt him shiver as he pulled her even closer. He bent forward and kissed her ear, lingering for a while before taking the lobe between his lips. He brought his kisses down onto her cheek and then gently, very gently, onto her mouth. She felt her legs go weak as she responded to the long, passionate kiss. And she told herself, Careful,

Jackie. Don't get carried away. This is just a holiday romance!

She found Caroline, slumped in one of the chairs on the veranda, her make-up streaked with tears, clutching a damp Kleenex.

She sat beside her.

"Oh, Caroline," she said. "Don't. He's not worth it."

"I feel dirty," sobbed Caroline. "He's dumped me like some piece of cheap trash."

Jackie resisted saying "I told you so."

"How can people be so cruel?" she continued to sob.

Jackie thought of Glen and said nothing.

Caroline gave one long howl and buried her face in her hands. "I want to go home!" she said.

Jackie was horrified. "*Home* home? Or hotel home?"

"I want to go back to the hotel," she sniffled. "I want to go to bed."

"Shall I get you a taxi?" asked Jackie, who couldn't bear the thought of leaving Mason just as things were looking so promising.

Caroline took Jackie's hand and gripped it tightly. "Come with me, Jackie," she pleaded. "I don't want to be alone."

"I'm sorry, Mason," she said. "You do understand, don't you?"

"No. Not really," he replied. "You're not her minder, you know. She's perfectly capable of getting a taxi back to the hotel on her own."

Jackie watched the pathetic figure of her friend, head hung low, making her way down the staircase.

"I've got to go with her, Mason. She's ever so upset."

She hoped that Mason would offer to accompany them home. Then he and Jackie, once Caroline had gone to bed, could take a quiet drink in the hotel's bar. There was no offer.

He reached out and squeezed Jackie's hand. "Whatever you feel's best," he said flatly. "I wouldn't want to come between you and your friend."

She resisted asking, "Shall I see you tomorrow?" though she longed for *him* to ask *her*.

He didn't.

"See you around," he said.

Jackie forced a smile and caught up with the bedraggled Caroline, dragging her tearful body down the staircase.

Glen was waiting for them as the taxi pulled up outside the hotel.

"This is all we need," whispered Jackie, expecting Caroline to react in the same way.

Caroline unexpectedly fell into the hairy arms and buried her face in his broad chest.

"Oh, I'm sorry, Glen," she bawled. "I'm sorry. I didn't mean what I said. Can we start again?"

Jackie stared, dumbstruck, as the relieved Glen enfolded her in his arms, grinned from ear to ear and then kissed the tear-streaked face.

"Of course we can," he said.

Arm in arm and oblivious to Jackie's presence, the reunited lovers ambled happily towards the bar to order a nightcap.

Jackie watched them disappear before going up to her room.

7

Jackie woke at six o'clock, disturbed by the noise coming from the bathroom. She heard the plug being pulled and the gurgle of water which followed. She sat up as Caroline emerged through a cloud of steam, towel-drying her hair.

"Sorry," said Caroline. "I tried not to wake you."

Jackie yawned and stretched. "Have you just got in?"

"No."

She crossed to her wardrobe and began sifting through her clothes, taking out several blouses, skirts and swimsuits and laying them on the bed.

"You'll never believe it," she said. "But I'm going to be a model for the day."

Jackie climbed out of bed and approached her.

"What d'you mean, a model?"

"David Brinkley is photographing Kristie on Paradise Beach today," she burbled excitedly. "It's a test-shot for Duane's album cover. And he wants a couple of blonde girls in bikinis to be in the background."

"And he's asked *you*?" Jackie wasn't surprised that Caroline, with her good looks, should be asked to pose for pictures, but she *was* surprised that she knew nothing about it. "When did this happen?" she asked.

Caroline picked up the white bikini. "Last night," she replied, adding, "D'you think I should take this one? It's a bit too revealing isn't it?"

"Last night? *When* last night?"

As far as Jackie was concerned, Caroline had spent most of the previous night bawling her eyes out on the terrace of Fantasma.

"I'll take it, just in case," said Caroline. "But I think the blue one's a bit more respectable."

"*When* last night?" Jackie repeated.

"Glen and I had a couple of drinks in the hotel bar," explained Caroline, "and then we decided to go back to the disco. I wanted to show Duane Sheldon that I didn't need him." She giggled nervously, noting that Jackie was displeased, to say the least. "You'd have laughed Jackie," she went on. "Glen and I danced beside Duane and that girl he was with all night . . . and he didn't take his eyes off me. He was really jealous. I bet he wished he could've dumped old Leather Skirt and gone off with me. Anyway, we got chatting to Mason Yellow Trunks . . . and you're right, Jackie. He's really nice."

Jackie felt her heart miss a beat.

"He was a bit upset that you hadn't come back to the disco, but I explained that you were tired and had gone off to bed."

Jackie was furious. "You *what*? I didn't know that you and Glen would be going back there. Why didn't you tell me?"

"I assumed you'd be asleep," said Caroline. "Anyway, don't worry. He wasn't angry or anything. He was just a bit upset. I think he thought he'd been dumped."

'Oh, God," sighed Jackie. Her eyes began to fill with tears.

Caroline put her arms round her. "Hey! Don't be daft," she said. "It makes you look really cool. He'll be even more interested in you now."

Jackie pulled away from her. "Sometimes, Caroline . . ." she said threateningly.

"Anyway, he then told me about this job and asked if I wanted to do background work on it."

She crossed to the mirror and checked her face. "I look like a pig," she said. "Look at these little scrunched-up eyes. I hope they open up before he calls for me."

"He's calling for you?" gasped Jackie.

"Him and David . . . and Kristie," replied Caroline. "And Duane, of course." She smiled. "Hey, don't worry. I'm not after your boyfriend, Jackie. Duane Sheldon's the only one I'm interested in."

Jackie flopped despondently on the edge of her bed.

"And what about Glen? What does he think about it?"

"He's a bit put out, of course," replied Caroline, "but he realizes that there's no future in our relationship. He's just got to accept that this is just a bit of holiday fun. Anyway, I told him that you'd take care of him today . . . and he was quite happy about that. I think he quite likes you, Jackie. You don't mind looking after him for me, do you?"

Jackie snapped. "Actually, yes . . . I do mind, Caroline. I'm going out for the day!"

"Where?" asked Caroline, surprised. "Where are you going?"

"I've no idea," replied Jackie. "But I'm not babysitting for you!"

"But Glen'll be calling for you at the usual time," said Caroline. "He's expecting to go to the beach with you. We've arranged it."

"Tough!" hissed Jackie as she flounced into the bathroom and locked the door behind her.

Caroline wished that she'd never agreed to do the test-shot. She hadn't realized that neither Duane Sheldon nor Kristie would be coming.

"Where is everyone?" she innocently asked David Brinkley as he greeted her in the hotel car park.

Mason sat behind the wheel of the Land Rover and a pale, tired-looking blonde girl, her hair in rollers, lolled in the back seat.

"It's only a test," explained David. "We just want to get the background shot right. We don't need the stars for that."

Deeply disappointed, Caroline climbed in beside the other blonde, who yawned and stretched, but said nothing.

"What did Jackie say?" asked Mason as he drove towards the main road. "Didn't she want to come?"

Caroline immediately began to feel guilty.

"She's taking care of Glen today," she replied.

Jackie skipped breakfast and ordered a taxi to take her into Santiago. She decided that this would be a perfect opportunity to shop for presents to take home for Mum and Dad. Caroline would have to sort out her own arrangements for shopping. She could do it later in the week ... with Glen. Or Duane. Or Mason!

Having bought a wood carving of an exotic-looking bird for her father and an exquisitely-mounted shell necklace for her mother, she crossed to the bar-café where she and Caroline had huddled from the rain and been chatted up by Rupert the stockbroker.

The bar was empty and Jackie ordered a Coke. She sat outside at one of the pavement tables, eyeing the mixture of passing natives and tourists. She wondered how Glen would have reacted when he'd arrived at the hotel to find that she'd already left. And she wondered how Caroline would be getting on with Mason. And she felt her stomach lurch.

Once the yawning blonde model had removed her rollers, combed out her hair, made up her face and struggled in and out of several swimsuits before David Brinkley had decided on the tiny black bikini, contrasting with Caroline's white one, the top photographer left the girls in Mason's control and climbed back into the Land Rover.

"I've got to pick up Kristie and Duane before nine o'clock," he said. "I'll see you later."

Caroline's excitement rose. "Are they coming to see the shoot?" she asked Mason.

Mason grinned, watching Caroline's face begin to flush.

"Nope," he said. "'Fraid not. David's taking them to Santiago . . . to look for some new outfits."

"Where d'you want us?" drawled the sleepy blonde model, eager to get started. "I'm only booked until lunchtime, you know."

Mason responded angrily, which surprised Caroline. She hadn't seen this side of him before.

"So? Have you got another booking this afternoon, then?"

"No," glared the model.

"So if you run into overtime, I take it you won't complain?"

"Where do you want us?" she repeated, staring at him through her just-opened eyes.

Caroline immediately began to wonder how much this professional model would be earning for the job. No fee had been mentioned to *her*. When she'd thought she'd be in the company of Duane Sheldon for the day, the thought of payment hadn't entered her head . . . but now?

"Let's start with the two of you leaning against that palm, gazing out to sea," he suggested. "You'll have to imagine that Duane and Kristie are frolicking in the water."

The model headed towards the palm-tree and

took up a pose, pouting sexily. Caroline studied her and did the same.

Jackie jumped when the Land Rover screeched up outside the bar-café, honking its horn. She looked up at David Brinkley's smiling face and was surprised to see Duane Sheldon and Kristie sitting in the back.

"You should be lounging on a beach!" laughed David. "Not hanging around bars!"

Jackie approached them. "What are you doing here?" she asked. "I thought you were all doing a photo shoot?"

"Too busy," grinned David. "I've left Mason to do it. Don't worry. Your friend Caroline's in very capable hands."

"I'm sure she is," replied Jackie, without grinning back.

"Let's have a break!" called Mason. "Time for some lunch."

He crossed to the pile of photographic equipment and grabbed the cool-box. "How about some pâté and champagne?"

"Sounds good," giggled Caroline. "Can I have a swim first? I'm sweltering."

The model sighed and glowered at her. "And what about your make-up and hair?" she tutted.

"Better wait 'til we've finished the shoot," agreed Mason. "We shouldn't be long. Another hour or so."

"I'll miss out on the eats, if you don't mind,"

slurred the model. "I'm exhausted. I'm going to have a snooze."

She slumped where she stood, beneath the shade of the palm-tree, and closed her eyes.

Mason humped the cool-box to the water's edge, stripped down to the famous yellow trunks and sat with his toes in the sea. Caroline joined him.

He opened the box, cracked open the champagne and poured some into two polystyrene cups, handing one to Caroline.

"Cheers!"

"Cheers!" she replied.

"Pity Jackie didn't want to come," he said. "I know we couldn't have used her for the shoot, but at least she could have supped champagne with us."

Caroline didn't reply.

"Shame she's not blonde," he added. "I'd rather have used her anyday than the Sleeping Beauty. Isn't she a pain?"

"I assumed all models were like that," replied Caroline.

"No. Kristie's charming. She'll work her butt off for the right shot. That's how she's got to her position. It's not just her beauty. There's more to this game than just looking good, believe me."

"D'you think I'd make a model?" asked Caroline. She sipped on her champagne, waiting for what she was sure would be a positive response.

"Seriously?"

"Of course, seriously."

"Forget it," he said. "To be honest, Caroline, they're two a penny. Unless you're very lucky, you'll spend most of your time struggling across London for casting sessions, competing with hundreds of girls, all trying to make a crust."

"What about America?" she asked naively.

"That's worse," he said. "Most of the models there have their eyes on the film world. They all want to be movie stars. At least in England there's no film industry anymore . . . which means everyone's given up trying."

"Oh," she said disappointedly.

"What do you do for a living?" he asked.

"I don't," she said. "Not yet anyway. I'm about to start work as soon as I get home. A cashier."

"A bank?" he enquired.

"A supermarket."

"Really?"

"It won't be for long, though," she added. "Not if I can help it. I'd like to find someone rich and famous and get married."

Mason almost choked on his champagne.

"Married? But you're far too young to get tied down."

She laughed. "Now, Duane Sheldon would be perfect!"

"But—"

"I know what you're thinking," she said. "What am I doing with Glen, when I've got my eyes on Duane."

He shrugged. "It's got nothing to do with me."

"But you don't approve."

"Just call me old-fashioned," he grinned.

She ran her eyes across his tight chest noting the tiny pool of sweat which had gathered there.

"I suppose I am a bit of a flirt," she said. "There's no harm in it. After all, I *am* on holiday. And if you can't have a little flirt when you're away from home . . . well . . ."

She saw that he wasn't smiling. She could see the pulse in his stomach beating rapidly. He was obviously getting excited by her flirtatious remarks.

"While the cat's away . . ." she smiled. She leaned across and gently placed her fingertips into the pool of sweat on his chest, ". . . the mice will play."

He removed her hand and playfully slapped it. "Not this mouse," he said.

He turned to face her. She was clearly embarrassed.

"More champagne?" he asked.

Jackie had taken her seat in the dining-room. It felt odd to be eating alone, but the waiters proved to be more attentive than usual, obviously feeling sorry for the redhead who had been left on her own. Caroline had returned from the shoot, found Glen waiting for her in the hotel bar and had immediately accepted his invitation to dinner in one of the upmarket restaurants in Santiago.

"You don't mind, do you, Jackie?" asked Caroline as she raced through the shower, leaving Glen to thumb through the magazines on the bedside table.

"Why should I mind?" replied Jackie, who was getting used to being left to fend for herself.

"I won't be home late," she said.

Glen looked up from the magazine, obviously disappointed by the statement.

"I'm very tired, Glen," she said. "It's been a long day."

"How did it all go, then?" asked Jackie. "How was Mason?"

Caroline shrugged. "It was OK. And he's all right, I suppose. Not that I can see what you see in him."

As Caroline left the hotel, arm in arm with Glen, Mason arrived.

"Is she about?" he asked.

"Jackie?"

"Who else?" he grinned.

"She's sitting in the dining-room, all on her lonesome."

"Then I'll join her," he said.

Caroline suddenly looked like a frightened rabbit. "I'll catch up with you, Glen," she said. "I just want a quick word with Mason."

Glen walked to the car and Caroline grabbed Mason's arm, dragging him to a quiet part of the hotel lobby.

"You won't say anything, will you, Mason?" she asked desperately.

"What d'you mean?" he replied, wide-eyed.

"You know."

He kissed Caroline on the cheek. "Go out and enjoy yourself," he said. "As far as I'm concerned, it's not even worth discussing."

"Thanks, Mason," she smiled.

* * *

"May I sit here?" he asked.

"Mason!" Jackie's face reddened.

"May I join you for dinner?"

"Of course," she said. She felt her heart racing. This was the last thing she'd expected.

"I've got a small proposal to make," he declared. "If you're not interested, then I won't be in the least offended. You've only got to say."

She had no idea where he could be leading. "Tell me."

"How do you fancy a little trip tomorrow?" he asked. "Just you and me?"

8

Jackie left Caroline a note, propping it up against the dressing-table mirror, where she would be sure to find it. Dressed in jeans and trainers and topped with her light-weight, cream-coloured blouse, she then noted the unusually cloudy sky and decided to take her jumper — just in case. This she pushed into the bright orange duty-free carrier-bag. Then, wondering if they'd be swimming or lounging on a beach somewhere, she added her shorts, swimsuit and beach towel. On top of this she placed her make-up bag, her hairbrush and an almost empty bottle of high-protection sun-oil.

The phone rang as she was pondering whether to take along her romantic novel.

"There's a Mr Wright waiting in reception."

"Thanks," said Jackie. "I'll be right down."

She squeezed *A Stranger Love* into the bulging duty-free bag and hurried to greet her date.

*   *   *

"A change of plan," said Mason as he wrapped his arm round Jackie's shoulder and kissed her on the cheek.

She immediately wondered if he were cancelling their date and she couldn't hide the feeling of disappointment.

"Not that it matters," he added, "considering you didn't know what the original idea was anyway."

He led her to the car park where a taxi, meter ticking over, was waiting.

"We're going a bit further afield than I first thought," he said. "It's David's idea and I leapt at the chance."

They climbed into the back seat, pushing Mason's heavy holdall to one side.

"Would you like me to put that in the boot, sir?" asked the black driver, looking in his rear-view mirror.

"No. It'll be fine," replied Mason, adding, "Can you take us to the port, please?"

The driver sounded surprised and delighted at the prospect of such a long distance fare. "El puerto?"

"El puerto. Sí."

Mason put his arm round Jackie's shoulder as the taxi made a three-point turn and trundled out of the car park towards the main road.

"Why are we going to the port?" she asked.

Mason laughed. "We're going on a boat trip, that's why," he replied. "I hope you don't suffer from sea-sickness."

"I've no idea," giggled Jackie. "I've only been on a boat once. The Woolwich Ferry."

The port of San Luis, situated on the south coast, was an hour and a half's car journey across Lacruz. Only once did Mason remove his arm from round Jackie's shoulder and this was done simply to get the feeling back into his numbing fingertips.

They talked and talked as they sailed smoothly through flat sugar-cane country on well-constructed tarmac roads, bumped their way up the steep mountain passes, surrounded on both sides by orange and lemon trees, took breath-taking swerves around hairpin bends through the banana plantations and slowed almost to a halt through several of the narrower village roads where goat-herders and their flocks took right of way.

As the taxi finally approached the outlying farmhouses of San Luis, Jackie felt she knew Mason better than she'd known anyone outside her own family, with the exception of Caroline of course. He'd talked so freely of his own background; his education and his past loves.

"I'm a romantic," he said. "It's the Spanish blood in me."

"Spanish? With a name like Wright?"

"My father's from Mormon country," he explained. "Utah. But he moved to LA when he was a teenager and married Conchita Paloma Alvarez, a Spanish beauty."

"So you speak fluent Spanish?"

"Sure do. My mother handed me down her language and her good looks." He laughed and squeezed her more tightly.

She grinned. "I can't argue with that," she said as she turned her face to stare into his smouldering, dark eyes.

He kissed her. A sweet, non-lingering kiss, before removing his arm once again from round her neck and placing his hand on hers, where their fingers affectionately intertwined.

He turned to look out of the window. "We're here," he said.

The taxi wound its way through the streets of single-storey, green-shuttered houses where the smiling black faces of the children, mostly bare-footed, seemed to greet them on every street corner. Whoops of joy filled the air as the innocents kicked footballs and turned skipping-ropes and wrestled playfully on the dirty pavements.

"Don't they go to school?" asked Jackie, checking her watch and realizing that it had gone ten o'clock.

Mason looked puzzled and called to the driver, "Why aren't the children at school?"

The driver grinned back in his mirror.

"Fiesta," he said.

Mason raised his eyes to Heaven. "I might've known." He gripped Jackie's hand more tightly. "They're on holiday," he explained. He appeared worried.

"What the matter?" enquired Jackie.

"It's a fiesta . . . which could cause us a bit of a problem."

As Mason had suspected, the quay was lifeless. More boats than ever had been docked, bobbing up and down on the calm water, their landing ropes secured.

"Nothing moving today by the look of it," he told Jackie.

They crossed to the cabin which doubled, curiously, as a tourists' knick-knack shop and the port authority's enquiry desk. It was locked. Mason shielded his eyes from the glaring sun and pressed his face against the door's smoky glass, peering deeper into the cabin to see if there was anyone on duty.

He turned to Jackie and shrugged. "Not a soul," he said. Then, noticing a battered and mud-splattered Lacruzian police vehicle pulling into the port car park, he hurried across to question its occupants.

Jackie heard the incomprehensible rattle-babble of Spanish and waited, once the police-car had moved on, for a translation.

"Nothing!" sighed Mason. "It's San Luis's second biggest fiesta of the year. Everyone's taken the day off."

"So does that mean we can't go on our boat trip?" asked Jackie.

"Well . . . *I've* got to go," said Mason. "This is a work trip for me, remember. It's not just a day out."

Mason had explained on the journey from the hotel that he was on a 'recce' for David Brinkley – that he had to reconnoitre the tiny island of La Luna for any particularly interesting locations, useful for photo-shoots, either for the job in hand or for future assignments.

"So you've got two choices," he proffered. "We can take you back to the hotel and start the trip again tomorrow . . . or we can spend the night here and set sail first thing in the morning."

"But where would we stay?" asked Jackie. "And what about Caroline? She'll be worried. I wrote her a note saying I'd be back tonight."

Mason laughed. "We're not totally cut off from civilization," he said. "They've got hotels here. And we can call the reception desk at the Maritimo and leave a message for Caroline."

Jackie placed her carrier-bag in her right hand and with the other she took hold of one of the handles on Mason's heavy holdall.

"So, what are we waiting for?" she asked. "Let's find a hotel."

Between them, they carried the holdall through the port car-park and back into the town. The streets were now empty, most doors of the houses remaining open or at least ajar to welcome a through breeze, should one occur. Jackie's legs were running with sweat and she couldn't wait to settle into a hotel room and change from her jeans into her shorts.

The Estrada Hotel was full.

So was Las Golondrinas.

"We can try the hostel over there," suggested Mason. "It won't be as good as a hotel but it's all that's left. If *that's* full we'll *have* to go home."

The hostel had plenty of vacant rooms which didn't surprise Jackie when she saw the squalor that faced her. Hers, next door to Mason's, was cell-like. An airless area just big enough for the single bed to fit. There was no cupboard space of any kind, so she emptied the contents of her carrier-bag onto the whitewashed, stone floor. She knelt on the nylon-sheeted bed and pushed open the shutters, peering down at the enclosed patio below which was home for the hostel's rubbish bins. One of the large bins had no lid and the garbage — an appetizing mixture of soft, yellowing lettuces, half-rotten tomatoes and stinking fish-heads — spilt out onto the floor and was being ravenously devoured by a mangey, cotton-thin cat with one frighteningly large, opaque eye.

"Not too good is it?" said Mason from Jackie's open door.

Jackie leapt down from the bed, grinning. "Totally luxurious," she giggled. "I just knew you'd bring me somewhere really romantic, Mason."

He laughed. "And they've given you the biggest room," he said.

He took her hand, led her past his room and down the corridor. "Just come and look at the bathroom. You'll love it."

He opened the door to reveal a grey stone-walled room.

Jackie felt the sun beating down and raised her eyes. "There's no roof," she said. She continued to gaze up at the cloudless, blue sky. "Where's the roof?"

"No roof," smiled Mason.

Jackie looked round the room.

"Where's the bath?"

"No bath."

"Shower?"

"A cold water pump behind that plastic curtain thing."

"The loo?"

He pointed to a hole in the floor.

"You've got to be joking," gasped Jackie.

"I wish I were," shrugged Mason in despair. "But there you have it! That's the bathroom!" He put his arm round her waist. "Would you prefer to go back to the Maritimo? I don't mind. Really I don't."

"No," replied Jackie. She laughed loudly. "Who needs a loo when you've got a hole in the ground?" She noted that on the wall someone had scrawled something in Spanish. "What does that say?" she asked.

Mason grinned. "Loosely translated it says, 'A thing of beauty is a joy for ever'!"

A voice behind them made them jump. "If you want lunch," said the hostel's proprietor, "we have a small dining-room in the annex."

"Thanks," replied Mason. "But I think we'll eat out."

To make amends for their living conditions, Mason chose what appeared to be the most expensive restaurant within the vicinity. Nearing two o'clock, the town was again beginning to come to life. The restaurant was almost full and its diners were extremely noisy. There were cat-calls and good-natured mock insults to the waiters and every fifteen minutes or so a family group or a gathering of friends would start to clap and burst into song.

"I wish I could understand what they're singing," said Jackie. "It sounds a real laugh."

"I can't understand it either," confessed Mason. "It's not Spanish. Well, it's not *quite* Spanish. It's a mixture of Spanish, English and Creole by the sound of it." He laughed. "Black Spanglish."

Jackie ordered a simple meal, feeling far too hot to eat any of the house specialities which Mason had warned her would be highly spiced.

"I'll have an omelette and salad, if they do it," she said.

"French omelette or Spanish omelette?" asked Mason, seriously.

"How about a Spanglish one?" laughed Jackie.

The waiter brought Mason the wine list and stood waiting to take his order.

"Are there any parades today?" he asked, enquiring further, "How do you celebrate the fiesta here in San Luis?"

"Es La Fiesta de Los Gumbos," replied the waiter.

Jackie stared wide-eyed, waiting for Mason to translate.

"It's the Fiesta of Los Gumbos, apparently," he said to Jackie. "Do you know what a gumbo is?"

"A gumboil?" she laughed.

"Gumbo. Gumbo," said the waiter. "A gumbo is the okra."

"Still no wiser," smiled Jackie. "Sorry."

"Okra is one of the main vegetables of Lacruz," explained Mason. "Here they call it a gumbo.

And today, it's the Fiesta of the Gumbo. A sort of celebration . . . religious I suspect . . . in praise of the gumbo . . . one of their main crops."

"Like Harvest Festival back home?" asked Jackie.

"You've got it," grinned Mason. "It's a sort of Harvest Festival for the gumbo." He turned to the waiter. "So let's celebrate your Fiesta de Los Gumbos with a bottle of champagne, eh?"

"Si Señor," smiled the waiter. "Coming up."

Feeling light-headed, although she'd sipped only one glass of the champagne, Jackie clung tightly to Mason as they followed the crowd, shuffling heel to toe, along San Luis's main street towards La Plaza del Obispo. The old town square, with its decaying fountains pumping out light brown water, was dotted with palm-trees in which there perched dozens of brightly-coloured birds. On the far side of the square sat the only noteworthy building of the town — the Church of San Luis. Its walls had recently been cleaned and garlanded with exotic flowers: alamunda, anthuriums and wild orchids.

The noisy throng soon filled the square, all eyes on the church, children high up on their parents' shoulders, the smaller adults on tip-toe, peering across the taller heads which blocked their view.

At five o'clock precisely, the church bells began to sound out and this was immediately acknowledged by a throaty roar from the crowd. The roar subsided as the bells stopped ringing and an eerie silence fell on La Plaza del Obispo. The slow beat of a solitary drum resounded from the church and the crowd watched in awe as a bejewelled float, carried on the shoulders of the priests, made its way from the church portal and down the ramp towards them. Men, women and children, crossing themselves, parted as one, without taking their gaze from the float as they made an inroad, through which the priests could carry their burden.

On the float, hundreds of candles burned brightly around the seated diamond-studded figure of the Madonna, and as the priests marched slowly through the crowds in time to the beating drum, an infant, following on behind, his black face smiling through his white, priestly robes, proudly carried on a silver platter the reason for this fiesta – the gumbo.

The almost silent religious procession which had taken two hours to wind its way solemnly through the side streets of San Luis, finally returned to the church, the gumbo having been buried, laid to rest in El Jardin de Los Santos, the equivalent of a small, English park.

The carnival followed: steel bands beating out their hypnotic rhythms in the square, while rum-crazed adults and their excited offspring danced wildly with police and priests.

As it grew dark, everyone returned to El Jardin de Los Santos to watch los fuegos – a magnificent firework display, its loud bangs echoing through the narrow streets nearby and sounding like thunder. Mason pulled Jackie closer to him and

93

held her tightly in his arms. And as the last rocket of the display shot high into the air, bursting and sprinkling the night sky with a thousand stars, he kissed her. And *that* was the kiss that she wished could go on and on for ever.

9

Even as early as eight in the morning, San Luis was buzzing. Jackie and Mason checked out of the hostel and sat at a pavement café, sipping very strong coffee. The celebrations were over and normality had returned to the town, the street cleaners having already removed most of the revellers' rubbish.

'This is my favourite part of the day in the Caribbean,' said Mason.

"Mine too," agreed Jackie. "Sunny, but not too hot."

"Not quite London, is it?"

"Not quite." She didn't want to be reminded. London was another world away – a world to which she had no desire to return. "I expect it's like this in L.A. though, isn't it?" she asked.

He laughed. "You have to be joking. We're lucky if we catch a glimpse of sun through the smog."

They finished their coffees and strolled down to the port, which was packed with cars and noisy natives queueing for tickets to other Caribbean destinations.

"Will there be many going to La Luna?" asked Jackie.

"I've no idea," replied Mason. "I know Lacruz like the back of my hand. *Should* do. We spent two months here on a calendar shoot last year. But I've never been over to La Luna. That's why David's curious."

Having paid for their tickets, they were pointed in the direction of a small motor-boat, engine purring, at the far end of the quay. Between them they carried David's hold-all towards the small gathering of people, three in all – the boat owner and two passengers – waiting to board.

"It's obviously not very popular," said Jackie.

The passengers were natives of Lacruz, both carrying identical sacks which obviously contained some sort of merchandise.

"Probably drug traffickers," whispered Mason with a grin. "We'll all be arrested and thrown into some dark Caribbean cell for the rest of our lives."

Jackie wasn't amused. She'd heard tales of supposedly innocent British girls being locked up in foreign prisons for drug offences.

Mason listened to the excited conversation between the two dreadlocked young men as they were helped aboard by the boat owner.

"Can't make out a word," he said. "I think they must have some sort of secret language which they use when there are foreigners around."

One of the passengers put down his sack and flopped onto the deck of the boat, grinning up at

Mason and Jackie and revealing a gold front tooth. The other stood at the boat's rail, looking out to sea.

"Hóla!" said Gold Tooth.

"Hóla!" replied Mason.

"English?" he enquired.

"American."

"The black, pitted face split into a wide smile. "American?"

"Yes. I'm American and my friend here is English."

"One English and one American," enunciated the grinning native.

"Yes."

"Una inglesa y un americano."

"Sí."

He stretched out on his back, placing his hands behind his head. "And why are you going to La Isla de La Luna?"

Mason shrugged. "Curiosity."

The man laughed.

"And you?" asked Mason.

"We take the drugs," he replied coolly.

Jackie suddenly began to panic. "Drugs?" she asked.

"Sí. The aspirin and the penicillin . . . and the Venos cough mixture."

"Oh! That sort of drugs," sighed Jackie.

The man sat up and stared at her. "Of course," he said, sounding surprised. "What sort of drugs do you think?"

Jackie gave a nervous twitch of a smile. "I don't know. I just . . ."

"The crack, eh?" he asked. He continued to stare at her, a comical look of mock-horror on his face. He smiled again, winked at her and lay back, chuckling.

The boat took only twenty minutes to arrive at the wooden jetty protruding into the sea from the rocky shore.

"Shame," said Jackie as Mason put out his hand and helped her step from the boat. "I thought it would be all sandy beaches and palm-trees like Lacruz."

"Me too," agreed Mason. "Looks a bit rough, doesn't it?" He put his arms round her waist and kissed her gently on the forehead. "What the heck? We can make it our own little paradise for the day."

Caroline was surprised to find the note, but felt pleased that Jackie was going out for the day with Mason. When the phone call came later that evening, Caroline was, luckily, just passing the reception desk, arm in arm with Glen.

"We're in a place called San Luis," Jackie had explained. "We were going to get a boat from here to a little island called La Luna, but there's a fiesta going on so there aren't any boats."

"So what are you going to do?" asked Caroline, immediately concerned. "Are you coming back to the hotel?"

Jackie felt nervous about telling her, wondering if Caroline would react badly to the news.

"Jackie? Are you still there?"

"Well, Mason suggests we stay the night here

in San Luis and get the boat across to the island first thing in the morning."

"And?"

"Do you think I should?"

Caroline laughed. "Of course you should. It'll be a laugh, won't it?"

Jackie fell silent, then half whispered, "He's lovely, Caroline. I feel very safe with him."

Recalling her visit to Paradise Beach with Mason, she replied, "He's really nice, Jackie. And I'm sure you can trust him."

Jackie lightened the conversation, "Hey, you should see the place we've booked into. It's really foul. And the people here are crazy. There's some sort of Harvest Festival going on and the people are loony."

"So are you calling from the hotel, then?"

"Hostel," corrected Jackie. "No. We're in this unbelievably posh restaurant and we're sipping champagne."

"Ooh, get you!" laughed Caroline. She turned to Glen. "Mason's taken Jackie to a posh restaurant and they're drinking champagne. I hope you're going to do the same for me."

Glen grabbed the phone. "We're going to a cheap café for a couple of lagers, Jackie," he said.

Jackie laughed as Glen handed the receiver back to Caroline.

"So you don't mind?" asked Jackie.

"Mind what?"

"That I won't be home tonight?"

"Don't be daft. Of course I don't mind. You enjoy yourself with lover boy. But take care."

"I will. You too."

"Don't worry about me," giggled Caroline. "I've got hunky Glen looking after me. I'll see you tomorrow sometime, eh?"

"Yes. Bye." She hung up.

"Well, she sounds ecstatically happy with Mason," smiled Caroline. "So let's see if you can make me just as happy, eh, Glen? Where are we going?"

"How about a posh restaurant where they serve champagne?" he laughed.

10

La Luna had no town, nor even a pueblo. Not far from the jetty stood a row of ramshackle buildings. Next door to the grocer's was the surgery and beside that was a small bar. The two sack-carrying drug transporters didn't take their wares, as would be expected, to the surgery. Instead, they leapt on to a small motorcycle propped up outside the grocer's, rode off along the narrow coast road and turned up into the hills, throwing up clouds of dust as they disappeared into the distance.

"Aspirin!" sneered Jackie. "I'm sure!"

They entered the small bar, stepping over a lazing, fawn-coloured, three-legged mongrel which was chained to the bars covering the dirty windows. The bartender, to their surprise, wasn't black. An overweight stereotypical Andalusian-Spaniard with an olive complexion and thick, black moustache, looked up and nodded.

"Sí?"

Mason ordered two Coca Colas and paid a very high price for them. They sat in the dark, sweltering bar, sipping their Cokes, too embarrassed to even whisper, knowing that in the silence their every word would be heard by the bartender.

Finally he crossed to them, using the excuse of wiping their table with a damp rag, to start up a conversation.

"English?"

Here we go again, thought Mason, giving the same reply as he gave to the gold-toothed Venos trafficker on the boat.

"I'm a photographer," explained Mason in fluent Spanish, "and I'm looking for interesting locations on La Luna."

The bartender was delighted at the American's almost-perfect Spanish accent. He pulled up a chair and sat at the table, directing some of his conversation to Jackie, although he'd been informed that she couldn't speak a word of his language. Playa del Oro it appeared was the ideal place for a photo-shoot: a rugged, beautiful coastline with a backdrop of red, crumbling cliffs housing dozens of caves.

"Perfecto!" enthused Mason. "How do we get there?"

On a carless island the only mode of transport, it transpired, was the motocicleta — a tiny two-seater pop-pop bike, which could be hired from the grocer. Mason negotiated what he reasoned to be a suitable hire fee and he and Jackie set off in the direction of Playa del Oro, following a rough sketch of a map drawn on the back of one of the Andalusian's beer-mats.

It wasn't easy passing over such rocky terrain whilst trying to balance Jackie's carrier-bag and Mason's holdall containing his camera equipment. Helmetless, shirtless and sockless ... and wearing just a pair of yellow trunks and trainers, Mason lightly gripped the handlebars and steered the noisy cycle up into the hills, following the tyre-tracks of their fellow boat travellers. Jackie, on the pillion and sweating profusely although lightly dressed in just shorts and t-shirt, wrapped her arms round Mason's bare waist and clung on, terrified ... and excited.

After thirty minutes of bumping over rocks and trying unsuccessfully to avoid the pot-holes, Mason finally stopped the bike.

"Time for a break," he called.

Jackie climbed off the saddle and Mason stood the bike against a tree and slumped at the edge of the road onto the dusty verge.

Jackie sat beside him. "It's not pretty, is it?" she said.

Mason looked behind at the fallen, decaying cherry trees covered with termite nests and the ailing sweet limes about to crumble. On the other side of the path stood a family of cactus.

"It looks as though it was quite something at one time," replied Mason. "But it's taken a battering from a storm, that's for sure. And talking of storms," he added, "I don't want to worry you ... but look!"

Jackie looked up at the black clouds beginning to gather above them. She smiled. "A bit of rain might cool us down," she said.

"It might," he smiled back. "Then again, it might drown us."

It started lightly and was indeed enjoyably refreshing, but as the drops began to get larger, Mason decided they should move on. They weren't, according to the map, too far from Playa del Oro.

The dusty path dropped and rose again like a roller-coaster; dropped lower, rose higher ... lower still and then ... up steep, steep, steep, until the bike reached a plateau which overlooked the whole of the south side of the island.

Jackie leapt from the bike and hurried to the cliff edge, noting the bright red soil beneath her feet, and looked down at the several winding paths which led through lush, un-windswept vegetation, to the palm-fringed golden beach below.

"This is better," she sighed.

Mason came to her side and took in the view.

"Playa del Oro," he explained, "is loosely translated as Golden Beach. And it certainly is!"

The rain was falling heavier now and Mason suggested that they take the nearest path down towards the beach.

"If that bartender was telling the truth," he said, "there are caves down there. It'll be somewhere to shelter if this turns into a real storm."

It was only as they struggled and slipped down the path, pushing the motorcycle, which was still laden with their bags, that Mason began to wonder if they'd made the right move. The rain now was torrential, the sky a threatening weave of black and mauve and bottle-green. The dust, now turning to mud, swallowed their feet up to the ankles with every step they took.

"I think we should go back," moaned Jackie.

Mason snapped, more from guilt than anger, "Don't be ridiculous!" He pointed upwards in the direction from which they'd come. "*You* try pushing the bike up there!"

He saw the shocked look on Jackie's face, stared at the wet, bedraggled red hair, the clinging t-shirt and the rain dripping off the end of her nose. He let go of the bike and went to her, wrapping her in his arms, pulling her closer to his bare chest.

"I'm sorry," he said. "It's all my fault. This is stupid. We should've sheltered up there, under the trees."

"It's all right," she replied softly. She shivered and snuggled into his arms, which wound round her more tightly. And she felt safe and comfortable. She gently pulled away from him and looked up into his eyes. "Mason, don't you think you should put a t-shirt on," she grinned. "I know you think you look like Tarzan . . . but honestly . . . you're so wet."

"Me? Wet?" He laughed and pulled her to him again. He kissed her ear and then whispered lovingly, "Me Tarzan. You Jane."

She turned her face and stood on tip-toe to whisper back into his ear, "You Tarzan. Me Jackie. And let's move on before we catch pneumonia."

He grabbed the bike and began moving faster down the path, giving a strangulated ape-call which was lost in the rain . . . and the wind, which was now beginning to rise.

Exhausted, they reached the shore, and here the wind was colder, the rain even heavier. They wheeled the bike across the damp beach, now not golden but burnt orange, and both leapt in horror as the fork-lightning shot from the sky and singed the sand just feet away. As the thunder boomed, they hurried on as fast as they could. Both sheet- and fork-lightning began to light the sky, the sheet lighting up the red cliff-face a few metres further down the beach.

"It's full of caves," gasped Jackie.

"Get on the bike!" yelled Mason, trying to top the thunderous roar from the heavens.

They mounted the motorcycle and sped along the beach, the sand beginning to harden with the heavy rainfall.

The first cave they came to appeared to be the biggest of the network of caves which covered the whole cliff-face, giving it the appearance, as the lightning flashed again, of a gigantic piece of Gruyère cheese. They wheeled the bike inside and leaned it against the wall of the cave, sitting beside it and staring out at the dark sky and the still water beneath it, lit every few seconds with a phosphorescent glow.

Jackie began to shiver and reached for her bag, taking out her beach towel and drying her hair.

"You'd better change," Mason suggested. "You can't sit around like that."

He kept his gaze on the beach, watching it dimple and crack and wash away as the rain fell on it. Jackie carried the bag to the back of the cave and changed into her bikini-top and her jeans and finally pulled the jumper over her head.

"That's better," she said as she came to sit beside Mason. "Now, what about you, Tarzan?"

He laughed, pecked her on the cheek and crossed to his hold-all. "Promise you won't look?" he grinned.

"Promise," she laughed.

He put on his dry t-shirt and swapped his shorts for his jeans. He returned to Jackie's side, shoeless, and put his arm round her.

"You all right?" he asked.

"Fine. Bit worried . . . but I'm fine."

"What are you worried about?" he asked, surprised. "You're in the company of Tarzan. What more do you want?"

She half-whispered, almost afraid to say, lest she appeared to sound foolish, "Did you notice the small cave above this one? The small one?"

"Why?" he replied. "You don't want to move house already, do you?"

"It had a rope-ladder leading up to it," she said.

He was silent for a while.

Then he spoke, softly. "I know. I saw it."

"So, do you think someone's up there?" she asked.

He shrugged. "Who knows? Still, if they have

their TV on too loud, we can always bang on the ceiling with the broom handle."

He spoke the words confidently, trying to cheer her with his humour. But she turned to face him just as the lightning lit the inside of the cave and she saw his worried expression.

"It's those men, isn't it?" she whispered. "Gold Tooth and his friend. The drug traffickers."

11

Caroline had felt curiously lonely without Jackie. It wasn't that she needed to be in Jackie's pocket all the time; indeed they'd spent a great deal of their time apart when Glen had accompanied them to the beach. But not to have her best friend there . . . to share her secret feelings with, to chatter over breakfast with, to discuss what clothes they should wear when they went out together in the evenings, was a trifle strange.

Glen had really pulled out all the stops when Jackie had talked of her luxurious meal with Mason. He'd taken Caroline to the Happy Lobster on the outskirts of Santiago and was grateful, when the bill arrived, that he'd taken his American Express card. The beautiful people of Lacruz dined here: the hotel owners and the richest of tourists. Caroline allowed the waiter to unfold and lay the heavy linen napkin on her lap as she eyed the room for celebrities. Where was

Joan Collins? Where was Princess Di? Glen too looked around and when his eyes fell on the stunning-looking girl with the long auburn hair and bright green eyes sitting at the next table, he was transfixed. Caroline had tried to laugh it off, telling him not to forget that he already had a date this evening, but in truth, she'd felt a pang of jealousy shoot straight into the pit of her stomach. And she didn't like it! Caroline had never before felt this odd emotion and she'd never understood how other girls at school had got so worked up when they'd discovered that their boy-friends had gone off with other 'dates'.

On the way back to the hotel she'd questioned him, trying to keep the voice light and giggly, not wanting him to realize that she was upset.

"What did she have that I haven't got?" she asked, as she snuggled up to him in the back seat of a taxi.

"Green eyes . . ." he grinned, ". . . skin as soft as silk . . . a figure to make Bimbo Blue Shorts look like Roseanne Barr."

"Well, perhaps you should've dumped me," she said, "and asked her out instead."

Wanting to tell her that there was no other girl in the world who could touch Caroline for her looks, that her personality was as sparkling as any he'd ever encountered, that beside her, ol' green eyes simply faded into plain Ms Average, but aware that given just an ounce of confidence Caroline could wipe the floor with him, he replied, "Did you see how much champagne she drank? I just couldn't afford her."

"But you can afford me?" She wasn't smiling.

"For the moment," he said.

The taxi pulled up at the Maritimo and Caroline expected Glen to climb out with her. He didn't.

"Aren't you coming to the bar for a nightcap?" she asked, sure that he was only teasing.

"No, I don't think so," he said.

Her face dropped. "But your car's here. Aren't you going to pick it up?"

"Too dangerous," he said. "I've had far too much to drink. I'll pick it up in the morning."

He stepped out of the taxi, kissed her quickly on the cheek and climbed back in again.

"I'll see you tomorrow," he said. "About ten."

She watched as the taxi pulled away, wondering where she'd gone wrong. Suddenly she knew she wanted him. This wasn't just a holiday flirtation. She put her hand lightly on her blouse and felt the rapid pulsating of her heart. Then she felt the tears sting the back of her eyes.

He's the one for me, she thought. Definitely. Unless it's just the champagne. No. She knew it wasn't that. For the first time in her life, she'd fallen in love. And the feeling excited her . . . and worried her. She was seized by panic. She'd fallen for him just as he'd begun to cool. How was she going to keep him interested? It would take a lot of careful planning.

As the taxi left the Maritimo's drive Glen sat back and sighed deeply. The temptation to go into the hotel with Caroline had been almost too much to cope with. He wanted to tell her how much he loved her. He wanted to hold her in his arms and kiss her and ask her what she felt for him. But he remembered the Duane Sheldon interlude. And he knew he had to be cool. If he weakened now, he was sure he'd lose her. And that would be too much to bear.

Jackie woke, wrapped in Mason's arms. She was surprised that despite her anxiety, she'd eventually drifted off to sleep. She found Mason staring at her and immediately worried that she may look unattractive when sleeping. Nobody had ever told her so, but then nobody had ever been this close. If she looked anything like her father, who always seemed to drop off in front of the television when Cilla Black was on, mouth opened wide, his face contorted with the pressure of his one fist pushed tightly under his chin, then Mason would surely have been put completely off her. She needn't have worried.

"Good morning, beautiful," he croaked, his eyes still half closed. He kissed the tip of her nose. "You've been sleeping like an angel."

She tried, gently, to pull away from him, feeling embarrassed that she'd allowed herself to get quite so intimate, without even being aware she'd done so. It must've been *he* who'd snuggled up to *her* in the night. She could remember nothing.

"Where are you going?" grinned Mason, gripping her tightly, not allowing her to slip away from him. "Don't move," he said plaintively. "This is great. You're all soft and warm." He kissed her forehead.

"How long have I been like this?" asked Jackie, now thrilling to his tightening grip.

"How long have you been snuggled into my chest?"

"Yes."

"All night," he lied, smiling. "You couldn't wait to get near me."

She knew it was untrue. At three in the morning she was watching him sleep, curled up with his back to her. She looked at her watch. It was only six o'clock now. But she pretended to believe him. She knew that his grip on her was so tight, that she couldn't pull away now, even if she were desperate to do so ... which she most certainly was not!

"I don't think I can move, anyway," he said. "I'm so stiff." He grinned at her. "My back, I mean."

"Me too. Not the most comfortable bed, is it."

They'd raked with their hands a small hollow in the sand and then managed with great difficulty to build up a sand pillow.

"It's my neck and my back," groaned Mason. "And my right shoulder and my leg and my ankle and my wrist and—"

"Shut up!" laughed Jackie. "Lie still and listen."

The gentle sound of water lapping on the shore and the screech of a distant gull was all they could hear.

"It's as though we're all alone in the world, isn't it?" said Mason. "You and me on a desert island. It's *The Blue Lagoon* revisited." He sighed, jokingly and spoke like an actor in an old Hollywood "B" movie. "It's just you and me, kid, with nothing but the sea ahead of us, the sand between our toes, the sky above our heads . . ."

Jackie laughed loudly. "Don't be stupid."

His stomach rumbled as he continued his speech. ". . . and nothing in our bellies." He suddenly pushed her away and sat up, still grinning. "Hey, kid, what are we going to do for food on this island? Can you fish?" He suddenly groaned and dropped his play-acting. "Ooh, my back."

Jackie pulled herself slowly to her feet. "Mine too. I ache in places I never knew I had."

"Last into the sea is a wimp!" Mason shouted. He tore from the cave and hurtled down to the sea. Dreamily she watched him go, realizing that she had, without doubt, fallen in love. And it hit her for the first time that it was nothing like *A Stranger Love* . . . it was nothing like the romantic novels she'd always enjoyed. This was the real thing. And it was such a strange emotion she was feeling. It was so exciting and yet at the same time it was so painful. Could this be why so many pop singers had crooned the sentiment, "Love Hurts"? It did! It actually hurt. And she realized this was probably because in her heart of hearts she knew this was just a holiday romance. In four days' time she'd be on the plane back to London, while he. . . ?

He paused at the sea's edge, ripped off his t-shirt and jeans and ran into the warm water, whooping his Tarzan call.

*   *   *

114

Caroline had raced back to her room after breakfast, hurriedly cleaned her teeth and packed her beach bag. She scurried out of the hotel, looking at her watch. It was nine forty-five. Glen would arrive at ten o'clock to find that she'd gone out. He'd enquire at the reception desk and be told that Caroline had informed them that she would be back soon, and would he please wait for her. On her return at ten thirty, he'd ask her where she'd been, obviously worrying that she'd met someone else and he'd show a little jealousy and this would mean he cared. And Caroline would win the first round!

She'd strolled along the beach and sat for a while gazing out to sea, hoping that Jackie was all right and that she and Mason were getting on well together. She couldn't wait to tell her best friend how she felt about Glen. She needed Jackie's advice and wished that she were here. Now.

She eyed her watch again and seeing it was ten twenty she decided to stroll back to the Maritimo. She'd see Glen waiting in the lobby and she'd say, "Sorry. I didn't realize the time."

She entered the hotel at ten thirty-five and was horrified to see that he wasn't there. Once again, just as it had the night before, her heart began to pound. Had he arrived . . . and on finding that she'd gone out, returned to his hotel? Perhaps he had another date lined up. She was about to ask the receptionist if there were any messages for her, when she saw Glen stroll in nonchalantly, with a wide grin on his face.

"Sorry, Caroline," he said. "I didn't realize how

late it was. I've been on the phone to London."

She crossed to him. "Your ex-wife?"

He laughed. "No."

She waited for a further explanation. There wasn't one.

"Ready for the off?" he asked. "I thought we'd try another beach today. I've got a map of the island and a guy at the hotel reckons there's a great beach called Las Dunas."

She tested him. "And suppose I say I want to stay here for the day?"

He tested her back. "Then stay. But I'm going."

She smiled. "I'll come with you."

Las Dunas was simple to find and the dozens of cars parked on the dirt track leading to the beach showed how popular it was.

"Probably too many people for comfort," said Glen. "If it's bad, we won't stay."

They ambled along the path, climbed across the dunes and faced the palm-dotted beach, not too crowded with tourists.

At the back of the beach was a small straw-topped hut where waiters were serving drinks and eats to those who preferred to sit in the shade, away from the blistering midday sun.

"OK for you?" he asked.

"Great," she replied.

They lay on their stomachs on the towel-covered rush mats they'd brought from the car, and felt the sun burn into their shoulder-blades.

"We won't be able to stay here for long," said Glen. "We'll fry."

Caroline placed the palm of her hand in the small of his golden-brown back. "You're burning already," she said.

He sighed. "That's nice."

She gently ran her hand up and down his spine, thrilling at touching the man with whom she knew she'd fallen head over heels in love.

"Ooh, that's really nice," he said. He turned on his side to face her, gazing deep into her eyes. "You're beautiful," he said.

Her stomach knotted. "And so are you," she replied softly.

He tried to stop himself from saying it, but the words blurted out, "I love you, Caroline."

He was shocked at her response. "I love you too, Glen."

He stared at her, hardly daring to ask, "What did you say?"

"I said I love you. I do, Glen."

He fell on top of her, kissing her passionately, squeezing her tightly.

And as she responded to his kisses, she heard the cracks of thunder, distant at first but rapidly approaching.

The sky turned from blue . . . to grey . . . to black and then the rain began to fall.

Caroline and Glen leapt to their feet, grabbed the towels, the rush mats and their beach bags and hurtled towards the refreshment hut where they were joined by dozens of sunworshippers all now jostling for a place in the overcrowded shelter.

* * *

Mason emerged from the water before Jackie, gathered up his discarded clothes and headed towards the cave with them, intending to place them in his holdall. He stopped when he saw the gifts which had been left at the entrance to the cave.

"What's that?" asked Jackie as she joined him.

There was a small bundle of twigs, a long metal skewer with a wooden handle, two fish and a bottle of water.

"A present from our neighbours, by the look of it," replied Mason. "Breakfast."

Jackie gazed up at the cave which, she suspected, housed the drug traffickers.

"So they can't be all bad, can they?"

Jackie knelt in the sand and examined the twigs. "They've even left us a box of matches," she said.

"Thank God for that," laughed Mason. "If I thought we had to light the fire by rubbing two sticks together, we'd eat raw fish ... or go hungry."

He knelt beside Jackie, took the matches from her and lit the fire, blowing on the sparks until they flamed. He then stuck the two fish onto the skewer and held them over the fire.

Jackie swigged at the water bottle. "I hope they haven't put drugs in this," she said, not being serious. "We could wake up in a few hours and find ourselves in some slave market, being sold off to the highest bidder."

Mason raised his eyebrows jokingly. "You're

getting worse than me," he said. He grabbed the water bottle from her with his free hand and gulped down half its contents. "Good of them though, isn't it? I wonder why they didn't come and give it to us personally?"

"Perhaps the fish is poisoned and we're going to be sacrificed to their gods."

"Laid out on a stone slab," continued Mason, "and our hearts cut out from us while they're still beating."

"Or we might be put on skewers like those fish and slowly roasted over an open fire," gasped Jackie. "They're probably cannibals."

Mason puffed out his chest in an attempt to imitate Sylvester Stallone. "They won't eat me. I'm too tough. But you, babe, are a different skewer of fish."

Jackie screeched with laughter, but stopped suddenly when Mason yelped, having burnt his fingers on the reddening skewer.

"You all right?" she asked, concerned.

He placed the skewer into his other hand and held out the injured fingers pathetically. "You'll have to kiss them better for me," he said, child-like.

She did. She kissed his fingertips lovingly. He leaned forward, lifting the skewered fish from the fire, and kissed Jackie on the lips. The kiss went on and on, growing more and more passionate. Suddenly he pulled away. "Mmm, that's made me feel really hungry," he joked. "Let's eat!"

He carefully removed the first fish from the skewer and handed it to Jackie. "No plates, I'm afraid," he said. "And no napkins. You just can't get the service nowadays!"

Jackie bounced the hot fish up and down in her hands, blowing on it, trying to cool it before taking a bite.

"It's still got its head on," she grimaced, staring at the creature's tiny, roasted and popping eyes. "I hate fish with their heads on."

"I expect they feel the same way about you," grinned Mason as he took a huge bite, sending fish oil rolling down his chin. "Mmm. It's very tasty," he said. "Better than eating cornflakes for breakfast, any day."

They were silent as they finished breakfast, Jackie handing half her fish to Mason.

"Right," said Mason. "Shall we do the washing up?"

Jackie laughed and lay back in the sand. The fire had died right down and Mason put out the glowing embers by kicking sand all over it. He then lay beside Jackie.

"I wonder what state the road is in?" he said. "I hope after all that rain, that there's still a road left."

"It's probably a river by now," she replied.

"Don't joke," he said. "You may well be right. If it is, we're stuck here."

She was excited by the thought. "For ever and ever?"

"And ever and ever, Amen."

He stood. "I'd better go and check it out."

"I'll come with you."

"No. You stay here," he said. "I won't be a minute."

He ran along the beach and leapt up the path which had led them to this beach during the storm. She watched his handsome brown body and the yellow trunks disappear then, with a contented sigh, she lay back on the sand and closed her eyes.

As the waiters dashed around, moving tables and chairs away from the drips which were leaking through the straw roof, the huddled holiday-makers, bodies running with a mixture of sun oil and rain water, began to shiver. Most grappled in their bags for shirts and blouses.

"I can't believe we were baking up in the sun just half an hour ago," said Caroline.

They watched the lightning strike the sea several times and waited for the loud booms of thunder which followed.

"I hope it doesn't strike this hut," said Glen, looking genuinely concerned. "We wouldn't stand a chance."

"Perhaps we should make a dash for the car," suggested Caroline. "We can't get any wetter than we already are."

Glen laughed. "You wanna bet?"

A waiter suddenly yelped and a young woman screamed as a section of the straw roof fell in, bringing torrents of water with it.

"Struck by lightning, or drowned?" asked Glen. "What would you prefer?"

"Neither, thank you," Caroline replied.

"Then let's go!" he yelled.

He raced out of the hut, hastily followed by Caroline.

They ran, screaming with mock-fear, along the beach, watched by the waiters and the other holiday-makers. Some decided to follow. Others stayed huddled together trying to find a dry spot under the now dangerously-sagging roof.

"They'll never be able to move their car," said one knowingly. "They should've stayed. It'll soon pass over."

Jackie awoke some two hours later and although watchless, she knew that it hadn't been just a five-minute nap she'd taken. She looked around for Mason and immediately began to panic when she realized he hadn't returned. She raced to the cave and pulled on her now dry shorts and t-shirt, checked her watch and sped along the beach and up the path, following in Mason's footsteps.

Puffing and sweating, she reached the top and saw with horror that her jokey prophecy had come true. The road was a small river which seemed not to move in any particular direction. There was no way it would just flow away, down to the sea. It would take hours, maybe days of very hot weather to dry it up. And if there were storms threatening to break, then Jackie feared that she and Mason would never get back. Without a boat of some kind, it would be impossible to travel, unless they were able to swim all the way back to the quay where they'd arrived from Lacruz. But then, there were the bags and the bike. Swimming was not an option. She wondered if the higher, wooded ground on the other side of the river offered some way through. And then she realized that this is what Mason must have gone to investigate. But why hadn't he returned?

Not even thinking about the danger, nor the fact that she was fully dressed, she plunged into the river and swam across, pulling herself up, with some difficulty, onto the far bank. Her heart began to beat rapidly, in sheer panic, when she contemplated the worst — had Mason been hurt? Was he lost in the wood? Would she be stuck here for ever, without him? And what about those drug traffickers? A young woman alone, miles from any civilization, she was perfect prey.

She headed into the wood, pushing aside the bracken and calling out his name, "Mason! Mason!" There was no visible sign that he'd come this way. She moved on deeper into the shade. "Mason! Mason!"

She climbed over a fallen, rotting trunk, pushed aside an overhanging branch and stumbled on, tears beginning to sting her eyes. "Mason!" she cried out desperately. "Where are you?"

She almost stopped breathing when she saw the man step into her path. The black figure put out his hand to her and grinned, showing his large gold tooth. A reel of thick rope was wrapped round his arm.

"Por aquí!" he said. "This way." He wanted her to take his hand. She didn't. This was some ploy, she thought. He'd done something to Mason and was now leading her deeper into danger. He turned his back on her and walked on, glancing back over his shoulder. "This way. Your friend is stuck. I went to get the rope."

She knew she had no choice but to follow him. "He's all right," said Gold Tooth. "No problema."

Fifteen minutes of struggling through undergrowth brought them finally to a small cliff.

"Allí!" yelled Gold Tooth. "Up there!"

Jackie looked up to see the terrified Mason stuck on a narrow cliff edge.

"What are you doing up there?" she yelled.

"I slipped," he called back impatiently. "What do you *think* I'm doing up here? Bird watching?"

Jackie began to follow Gold Tooth as he clambered up the cliff.

"No!" he said. "Stay here. I don't want to rescue two persons."

He sped up the cliff edge like a mountain goat, finally reaching the cliff-top above the ledge on which Mason was precariously perched. He threw one end of the rope towards the ledge and Mason grabbed it.

"You'll never pull me up by yourself!" yelled Mason.

Gold Tooth grinned as every muscle in his black, lean body seemed to flex.

"No problema!" he yelled back.

Mason tied the rope tightly round his bare waist, and the powerful Gold Tooth pulled him, slowly, to safety.

As Mason ran down the cliff towards Jackie, following Gold Tooth who was now grinning wider than ever, he rubbed the rope burns round his waist.

"How embarrassing," he said as he wrapped an arm round her. "I was trying to play the hero and find a way out for us."

"But *I* am the hero," laughed Gold Tooth.

Jackie grinned at Mason. "He Tarzan. You Jane."

"Oh, thanks a lot!" replied Mason.

"Por aquí!" said Gold Tooth, leading the way through the trees. "This way!"

They followed him.

At the rope-ladder leading to Gold Tooth's cave they parted company.

"Tomorrow is possible be good for travel," said Gold Tooth. "We look at el río early to see if the water is dry up."

"I suppose it depends on the amount of sunshine we get today?" asked Mason.

"Exactamente!" replied Gold Tooth, adding, "Un momento." He shinned up the ladder to his cave and within a few minutes had returned with a string bag of groceries; salad stuff, eggs, potatoes and more water, this time in a large plastic container. "I'll bring some wood for the fire and some things for to cook with pronto," he said.

"Muchas gracias," smiled Mason.

"Thanks," added Jackie.

12

Jackie and Mason returned from their early morning swim to find Gold Tooth, dressed in jeans and a white vest, sitting outside their cave with another small bag of groceries and more firewood.

"You can't keep doing this," said Mason. "Surely you need all your provisions? You can't exactly call at the local supermarket every time you need a bottle of water."

Gold Tooth laughed. "We don't buy water. We have fresh water on La Luna."

Mason was surprised. "Fresh water? Where? Is there a spring?"

"I will show you later," said Gold Tooth. He began to build the sticks into a small fire, placing a crumpled piece of paper between them before reaching for his matches.

"All the food we get every two weeks from Lacruz . . . when the weather let us cross."

"So that's what you were bringing over on the boat," said Jackie.

"Sí. No drugs." He laughed. "Just tea-bags and other ..." he struggled for the English word ". . . comestibles?"

"That'll do," smiled Mason.

Gold Tooth lit the fire and blew on the tiny blue flame. "I will take breakfast with you," he said, handing them some eggs from the bag. "Who will cook?"

"I will," said Mason. He went into the cave to fetch the small frying-pan and other utensils belonging to Gold Tooth.

Gold Tooth took out three tin plates and some forks from his bag and placed them on the sand. Then he held out his hand to Jackie. "I am Fernandez," he said. "And my amigo is called Pedro."

"Jackie," she replied.

Mason approached with the pans. "And I'm Mason."

Mason poured some oil into the pan and cracked the eggs into it. They immediately began to crackle and spit.

"What made you decide to live here, Fernandez?" asked Jackie. "It must be a hard life."

"Hard life? No. It's not a hard life. It is easy. Life on Lacruz is hard with work, work, work."

"But how do you survive?" asked Mason.

Fernandez looked a little guilty. "I don't survive without Pedro," he explained. "Pedro is very rich."

Jackie and Mason were both surprised. They'd imagined that these two men whom they'd first met on the boat from Lacruz were vagabonds, forced to live this existence through lack of funds.

"Pedro had much land," went on Fernandez. "Many orange groves and a big hacienda. But he sold all. It is now El Maritimo."

"Really?" gasped Jackie. "That's where we're staying. The Maritimo Hotel."

Fernandez Gold Tooth grinned and shrugged. "Everyone stays at the Maritimo."

"So couldn't Pedro have bought more land on Lacruz, and lived in luxury?" enquired Mason.

"Sí. But he didn't want to. He like the life of the campesino. Lacruz is all British and Frenches and Germans." He grimaced. "No me gusta. I don't like. Lacruz need them. The people on Lacruz can now live better but only as slaves to the tourists. My land is now changed. It's more better here. The wife of Pedro prefer Lacruz. She stay. They made many arguments."

"So where is Pedro now?" asked Jackie. "Isn't he going to have breakfast with us?"

"He is working," replied Fernandez. "We will go to see his work when we have eat the eggs . . ." he nodded towards the pan, ". . . which are cooked."

Mason took the pan off the fire and served the eggs on the tin plates.

"I will take you to Pedro," said Fernandez, as he picked up a fork, "but first we eat, eh?"

They followed Fernandez along the beach and up the path towards the flooded road where, Mason observed, the water-level appeared to be lowering.

"One day more," said Fernandez. "It will be dry."

"Unless we have another storm," said Mason.

Fernandez nodded. "Correcto."

Taking a left fork at the side of the river, Fernandez began to climb the red cliff, checking every few minutes to see if Mason and Jackie were behind him. It was a steep, though straightforward climb to the plateau a few hundred metres above them. From the top the three of them stared down at the lush green forest on the other side. At the edge of the forest a wisp of smoke from a bonfire and a tiny figure of a naked black man caught their attention.

"Pedro no speaks English," explained Fernandez as they made their way down towards the bonfire. "And he very tímido."

"Shy," Mason corrected him.

"Sí. Pedro is very shy."

Pedro saw them approach and raced to his pile of discarded clothes, slipping on some ragged jeans.

Fernandez ran on ahead. "I will explain Pedro who you are," he called back.

As Mason and Jackie arrived at the bonfire, Pedro gave a flicker of a smile and a quick nod, before turning his back on the visitors and returning to his work.

"He's very shy," repeated Fernandez, as though apologizing for his friend.

A large area of woodland had been hacked down and the reclaimed land had been cultivated with various unrecognizable crops.

"We have enough vegetables here for to feed us," explained Fernandez. "There is a stream allí," he said, pointing ahead. "It has fresh water to fill our bottles every day. And we have fish from the sea." He grinned. "And of course, tea-bags and eggs and tinned meat from Lacruz."

"I suppose you trade what vegetables you don't need for your eggs and things do you?" asked Jackie naively.

Fernandez gave a bellow of a laugh. "No! Pedro takes money from the bank and he buy them."

He saw the look of disappointment on Jackie's face.

"Why make life difficult?" he said with a shrug.

He led them further into a field which had just begun to sprout tiny green shoots.

"What are these?" asked Mason. "Potatoes?"

"I don't know," grinned Fernandez. "I don't know nothing of the vegetables. My job is the fishing and the cooking. And soon we will get some chickens from Lacruz and have fresh eggs and fresh meat." He smiled at Jackie. "But I don't kill the chickens. Pedro must do that. I don't like to kill nothing. Even to kill the fish is not good for me."

Having inspected most of the fields, Fernandez had a quiet word with Pedro, who looked at his two guests and nodded amiably. The three of them then left the shy 'campesino' to continue with his work as they returned to the beach to wash their breakfast things in the warm water.

Using underwater snorkels belonging to Fernandez and Pedro, Jackie and Mason circled a

130

rock a few metres out to sea. The water there was shallow enough to paddle and therefore the abundance of brightly-coloured fish of all different shapes and sizes amazed the explorers.

Doggy-paddling, with her head just under the surface, Jackie noted a small hole in the side of the rock and took a further look. A sad-looking fish, its mouth down-turned stared out from the hole with its bulging eyes as if saying, "Please go away. I want to be alone." Jackie was about to turn away from the rock when something touched her leg. She almost swallowed water as she gasped, turning quickly to see what it was. Mason was running his fingertips up her thigh. He was grinning at her. She grinned back and grabbed his hand. He removed his snorkel and signalled for her to do the same, which she did. Then he held her tightly and kissed her.

From another nearby rock, Fernandez, fishing-rod in hand, watched the lovers stand slowly in the water, snorkels dangling by their sides, lost in each other's kisses. They heard him laugh loudly and Jackie pulled away, embarrassed.

"Sorry!" called Fernandez. He covered his eyes playfully with his free hand. "I don't see you. I am not here." He laughed again.

"Too late, Fernandez," Jackie laughed back. "You've spoilt the moment."

"Aah," he sighed. "True love cannot be spoilt so easily."

Jackie blushed and hoped that Mason hadn't noticed her reddening cheeks. She'd hoped he hadn't heard what Fernandez had said. The words 'true love' to somebody who just considered this to be a holiday fling, would send him reeling from her, she was sure of that. Mason grabbed her round the waist as they both paddled back to the shore.

"Plenty fish?" called Fernandez.

"Plenty!" Jackie called back. "And they're so beautiful."

"Nice to eat too," laughed Fernandez as he whisked his empty line from the sea and, disappointed, recast immediately.

"Did you hear what he said?" asked Mason as he and Jackie padded up the beach towards the pile of charred sticks which had been their fire. "True love," he said.

Jackie wasn't sure if Mason was about to laugh. She was wondering how she'd react if he made fun of the comment and quickly spared him the opportunity to do so.

"Did he?" she said. "Shall we get the fire going again and make some tea?"

A cry from the path startled them.

"Gumbo! Gumbo!"

They looked up to see Pedro, hurtling towards the beach with a vegetable in his hand.

He sounded crazed. "Gumbo! Gumbo!"

Fernandez placed his rod on the rock and ran towards his friend. Both inspected the vegetable excitedly and flung their arms round each other, dancing round and round in circles, shouting, "Gumbo! Gumbo!"

Jackie and Mason raced over to them.

"El gumbo!" explained Fernandez. "We try to grow the gumbo but it is difficult here because the ground is bad for gumbos. But look!" He grabbed the okra from Pedro and showed it to them. "We have success."

"It was probably something to do with the fiesta," said Mason, half-jokingly. "La Fiesta De Los Gumbos."

"Sí . . . sí . . . sí," replied Fernandez seriously.

"Sí! La Fiesta De Los Gumbos!" agreed Pedro.

Both men crossed themselves.

Then Pedro grabbed back the okra and whooping loudly, he scurried up the path to continue with his labour of love.

Having brewed some tea, Jackie went into the cave to fetch her sun oil. She'd been so careful all holiday, but for the first time she was beginning to feel sore. She'd used the oil sparingly since they'd arrived on La Luna, knowing that she had very little left.

As Fernandez and Mason sipped tea from the enamel mugs, Jackie squeezed what oil she could from the bottle.

"Oh!" she said. The bottle gave out a puff of air as she squeezed it again. "That's it! It's empty. I suppose I'll have to go and sit in the cave."

"You don't need the oil!" lectured Fernandez.

"*You* may not!" replied Jackie. "But I do. I burn very easily."

"I burn too," said Fernandez, his gold tooth glinting in the sun as he grinned at her. "But if the sun is very hot, I use the red dust." He took her hand and led her towards the cave. "Come."

Mason followed them.

Fernandez rubbed his hands on the red cliff face. Then he spread the dust all over his cheeks. He looked extraordinary – the bright red face atop the black neck and body.

"It's good for the skin," he said. He continued to rub the dust all over his body. "Do it," he said. "It will stop from burning."

Jackie was in two minds. She knew she needed protection, but felt she'd rather sit in the shade than end up looking as unattractive as Fernandez now did. How would Mason react to her if he saw her looking like a freshly boiled lobster? That would put him right off!

She felt relieved when Mason stepped forward, rubbed his hands in the red dust and then began wiping it across his face. Jackie immediately followed suit. They chuckled like children as they wiped the dust over each other's backs, until all three of them were completely covered; not a single inch of bare skin being offered to the sun's rays.

Fernandez returned to his fishing, promising to catch them something special for lunch, and Jackie and Mason lay back on the sand, arms wrapped round each other.

"You look more beautiful than ever," grinned Mason. "I've always loved tomatoes!"

Jackie hit him.

The drive back from Las Dunas to the Maritimo

was a treacherous one as Glen had to avoid rock-falls and flooded roads and even a burst water-main on the outskirts of Santiago. Throughout the whole time, the rain fell heavily, limiting his visibility through the windscreen.

They finally arrived at the hotel and fled, still in their swimming costumes, from the vehicle, across the car-park and into the hotel lobby. Many of the guests had been caught out in the same way and they crowded into the reception area, some with towels over their heads, all bemoaning the fact that the sunny Caribbean had let them down.

As Caroline waited for the key to her room, David Brinkley approached, calling, "Hi, you two! Been for a swim?"

Caroline grinned at him through her wet, straggling hair. "Very funny."

"Why don't I order us some coffee in the dining-room?" suggested David. "While you two go and dry yourselves off. I've got something to tell you."

Caroline was immediately concerned. "It's Jackie isn't it?" she said. "What's up?"

"There's nothing to worry about," replied David. "Join me as soon as you're ready."

He walked into the dining-room as the receptionist handed the key to Caroline.

"I was a bit concerned because Mason didn't check in with me last night," he explained. "I was expecting him back, but when he didn't arrive I at least expected a call from San Luis. Anyway, to cut a long story short, I called the San

Luis port authority office and they told me that La Luna, the island where he and Jackie have gone to, has been cut off in a storm."

"Cut off?" Caroline gasped. "D'you mean they're trapped?"

"Seems like it, yes."

"But how long for?" asked Glen. "The girls are going home on Sunday."

Caroline shivered. She didn't want to be reminded that in three days' time they'd be on the plane back to London.

"I've no idea," shrugged David. "I rang the port authority again this morning and it appears that the storm has passed over . . . but unfortunately there's another one on the way!"

Jackie had drifted into a deep sleep, feeling totally secure and happier than she'd ever felt in her young life. When she woke she saw Mason standing at the sea edge, his body now covered in red streaks where the dust had mingled and run with his sweat. In his hand was her empty sun oil bottle. She approached him quietly and watched him as he screwed the lid tightly onto the bottle and threw it into the water.

"What are you doing?" she asked.

He jumped and turned. "I thought you were asleep."

"I was."

"I've just written a little note and thrown it out to sea," he said. "Who knows, someone in some far off land may find it."

"A message in a bottle, eh?"

"Something like that," he replied, sounding rather melancholy.

"Asking for someone to come and rescue us?"

"No!" he said. "Definitely not. Why should I want to be rescued?"

He walked past her, his head hung low and made his way to the cave.

13

Jackie stood at the entrance to the cave, looking down towards the sea, where Mason, leaning on a palm-tree, seemed lost in thought. She'd slept so deeply and hadn't heard him wake. She strolled towards him.

"Penny for them," she said.

He turned and smiled at her. "Good morning, Princess. I was just thinking that if we don't move on today, we could find ourselves trapped here for weeks. Take a look at that sky."

Far out to sea, the sky was black, although, as yet, La Luna was bathed in warm sunshine.

"I'm not sure which way it's going," he said, "but if it's heading our way, then we're done for. That road will be impassable."

"Perhaps we should go and take a look at it," suggested Jackie. "If the water has dropped to a reasonable level, maybe we could paddle back."

"And what about the bike?" asked Mason. "We'd never manage to wheel that through flood water."

Fernandez came running, calling excitedly, "Mason! Jackie! The road is dry."

They looked up to watch him cartwheel across the beach. He stood on his hands and walked along on them, laughing. "I should be in a circus, eh?"

"He's quite mad," said Jackie.

"But harmless," grinned Mason.

With a final leap, Fernandez stood before Jackie and bowed. "Good morning. The road is dry," he repeated. "You can go home."

"You sound as though you can't wait for us to leave," said Jackie, pretending to be hurt.

"This is true," laughed Fernandez. "But first, we invite you to our home, for breakfast."

"Fish?" asked Jackie. "It's got to be fish."

"Or eggs," said Mason.

"Kellogg's Corn Flakes," smiled Fernandez. "With milk. Very English."

"American, actually," corrected Mason.

Fernandez began to lead them towards the rope-ladder which led to his cave.

"Where do you get milk from around here?" enquired Mason.

Fernandez didn't reply. He rapidly climbed the rope-ladder until he'd reached the narrow ledge which served as a doorstep to his cave. He indicated that Jackie should climb up next. Mason followed her.

"My home," said Fernandez, proudly. "Bien venido. Welcome."

They entered and were shocked and delighted at their surroundings. Light filled the whole area from an inlet at the rear of the cave. The floor was covered with rugs, the walls adorned with paintings. There were two hammocks for beds, supported by a tall wooden frame.

"I made that," said Fernandez.

"This is fantastic," gasped Jackie. "It's like a real home."

Fernandez frowned. "It *is* a real home!"

He showed them the kitchen area: a large 'cold' box, which he said kept food fresh for at least three days, a small stove operated from gas cylinders, rustic tables, chairs and cupboards, plate-racks . . .

"It's better than our kitchen at home," said Jackie.

"And why not?" chuckled Fernandez. "We are probably richer than you. The only thin' we don't have is the bathroom. But we got the Caribbean!"

Pedro entered from behind them, struggling with the only English he had. "Hello. I am happy to greet you."

Mason put out his hand to shake Pedro's, who was looking like a frightened rabbit.

"Hóla!" replied Mason. He started a conversation in fluent Spanish and Pedro responded warmly to the American.

"Pedro will have breakfast with us," Fernandez informed them. "And then he goes back to work. And you go home before the new storm."

"Do you think there *will* be a storm?" asked Jackie, concerned.

"Seguro," replied Fernandez. "For sure."

They sat around the table in a civilized manner

140

and ate cornflakes with fresh milk from the cold box, and Jackie couldn't help wishing, despite her earlier protestations, that for their last meal here on La Luna, they were eating fish, cooked over an open fire on the beach.

They followed the cornflakes with toast and apricot jam. And as Fernandez prepared instant coffee, Jackie crossed into the 'lounge' area to pick up the guitar she'd seen leaning against the wall.

"Whose is this?" she asked.

"Es mío," replied Pedro.

"He play very well," added Fernandez. "We play mucha musica," he grinned, "because we don't have the television."

Jackie began to play as she sang. And they all fell silent, listening to a perfect rendition of 'Homeward Bound'.

"I know this song," grinned Fernandez. "Pedro have played this song." He looked at Pedro, who was singing along, in perfect English.

"He don't understand what he sing," said Fernandez. "But he sing it good."

Pedro reached up to a shelf and took down a flute. This he played along with Jackie as Mason and Fernandez joined her in singing the Paul Simon lyrics.

Suddenly Jackie's voice seemed to crack. She stopped singing and looked up at the three men. Two weeks ago, in her other life, she hadn't known of their existence and now here she was, happier than she'd ever been, singing a song about going home. And leaving them. And she burst into tears.

Pedro approached her, flute in hand and put his arm comfortingly round her. He hadn't understood the significance of the lyrics, but he had seen the look between Jackie and Mason and he knew that the girl was in love.

"I'm sorry," sniffled Jackie. "That was very stupid of me."

Pedro held the flute out to Jackie. "Es tuyo," he said.

"He says it's yours," translated Mason. "He wants you to have it."

"Es un recuerdo," said Pedro.

"A souvenir of our meeting," explained Fernandez.

Jackie examined the flute, a beautiful, hand-carved instrument, with delicately painted pictures of oleander and humming-birds.

"It's stunning," sighed Jackie. "I can't take this."

"Pedro made it and painted it," said Fernandez. He smiled affectionately at Pedro. "He is in love with his flute."

"Then how can he think about giving it away?" she asked. "How can he bear to lose something he loves so much?"

Fernandez shrugged. "Will you love it too?"

"Oh, yes," replied Jackie. "Oh, yes!"

"Then Pedro will only be sad for a short time," he said. "And you will remember us always."

Wheeling the bike along the muddy road proved to be difficult, though both Jackie and Mason were surprised that the river had disappeared as rapidly as it had arrived. They moved as quickly as they could, eyeing the sky from time to time, aware that it was turning a nasty shade of grey.

"If we have another storm like the last one, we'll never get back to Lacruz tonight," said Mason. "It's cutting it a bit fine for you, isn't it?"

Jackie didn't want to be reminded. "We leave on Sunday," she said. "The day after tomorrow." Her thoughts immediately turned to Caroline. She must be worried sick by now. She wondered if Caroline and Glen would have contacted David Brinkley to find out where Mason had taken her. And she hoped that David Brinkley would have found out that there'd been a storm on La Luna and had told Caroline that there was no need to panic; that Jackie was in good hands.

"My flight's on Monday," said Mason.

"Are you going back to London before you set off for America?" she asked hopefully.

"Only to change planes," he replied. "All my worldly goods have already gone by sea."

She walked ahead of him, not wanting him to see the tears streaming down her face. She feared the emotion was showing in her voice.

"I don't really want to go now," he added. "I wish we could have a bit more time together."

She took a deep breath and croaked out the words, "Me too."

Ahead they could see the quay, though there was no sign of a boat to take them back to Lacruz.

"It's early yet," said Mason, looking at his watch. "Don't worry." He laughed. "We'll have a drink at that cute little bar and wait for it to arrive."

* * *

As the sun rapidly dried the Maritimo's flower-beds and the pool patio, the holiday-makers began to drift back to the terraces, all with their dramatic and exaggerated stories of how the storm had affected them. Glen and Caroline sat at the pool's edge, their feet dangling in the water.

"Did you mean it?" he asked, gazing down at the blue tiles on the bottom of the pool. "Did you mean what you said on the beach?"

She put her hand on his arm. "Yes," she whispered. "What about you?"

He lifted his head and turned to face her. "It's a bit frightening for me," he said. "I've been through all this before and . . . well, it makes you a bit wary."

"There's no need to worry, Glen," she assured him. "I meant what I said. I love you. I can't promise hand on heart that I'll always feel this way. Who can? But at the moment, I'm just so happy to be with you."

He put his arm round her.

"And I'll miss you," she added.

"Miss me?" He gently lifted her chin with his hand, forcing her to look him straight in the eye. "What do you mean, miss me?"

"When I go back to London," she replied.

"But I commute to London from Essex," he explained. "It's only a thirty-minute journey."

"I didn't mean . . ."

"So I can see you every day," he went on.

She laughed. "I know. I didn't mean that. I meant I shall miss you on Sunday."

He was puzzled.

"I go home on Sunday and you've got another day here haven't you?"

He grinned. "Oh, I see! You're worried about leaving me behind."

"Yes."

"Just in case I meet someone else in the twenty-four hours we're apart?"

"Well, you never know."

"Don't be daft," he said. He kissed her forehead. "Anyway," he added, "I'm going with you."

She was stunned. "You what?"

"That call I made to London," he smiled. "It was to my friendly travel agent. I've changed my flight. I'm travelling back a day early. On your plane."

She gasped and flung her arms round his neck. "Oh, Glen!"

"Let's swim!" he suddenly yelled. He leaned forward and fell into the pool.

With a squeal of delight, she tumbled in with him.

"So you didn't like Playa del Oro?" asked the barman with a wide grin.

Jackie was surprised to hear him speaking in English. On their previous encounter, the whole conversation had been conducted in Spanish.

"My wife is English," explained the barman when Jackie questioned him.

"Your wife? You have a wife?" Jackie was taken aback. She just couldn't imagine why any woman would want to spend her life on La Luna, totally cut off from the real world. It was even more surprising to hear that the wife was English.

"I talk English all the time to her," continued the barman. "She don't speak Spanish. I get sick of the English. Your friend spoke Spanish so *I* spoke Spanish."

"It's not that we didn't like Playa del Oro," said Mason. "On the contrary. It's beautiful. But we couldn't take the risk of filming there. We couldn't afford the luxury of wasting two or three days while we wait for flooded roads to dry up."

The barman gave them each a Coke, smiling, "It's on the house."

"Gracias," said Mason.

"Thanks," said Jackie.

"We don't have storms all the time," laughed the barman. "Only in September and October. If you come in June or July, we never have rain."

Mason sipped his Coke. "I'll let my working partner know that," he said. "It's got nothing to do with me from now on. I'm going home to the States on Monday."

Jackie's stomach lurched.

The barman turned to the doorway behind him and pushed aside the plastic curtain which covered it, calling, "Linda!" Then he turned back to face Mason and Jackie. "My wife. She likes Americans."

Jackie felt a pang of jealousy. She began to worry that Mason might have eyes for this new English woman who liked Americans.

"Linda means beautiful in Spanish," said the barman. "My Linda is the most beautiful woman on La Luna." He leaned forward, resting his elbows on the bar and whispered, "That's not difficult of course. She's the *only* woman on La Luna!"

Linda appeared, looking sleepy-eyed, an attractive fair-haired girl in her early twenties.

"Hi!" she greeted them with a gentle smile.

Jackie saw Mason look her up and down.

The rain started lightly at first and Linda had told them not to worry. The boat would arrive in all weathers, minus a storm of course and neither she nor her husband were expecting that to happen today. They were wrong. The lightning was still distant but occurring every few seconds and soon the thunder, at first a low throb, was now ripping across the channel towards La Luna.

"I don't think you'll get away from here today," Linda finally conceded. "This is going to be a bad one, I'm afraid."

As the storm grew in intensity, the barman, who introduced himself as Juan Jesus, decided that their rare visitors would be given a special lunch; paella, just like Juan Jesus's mother used to make, when they lived in Cordoba. Linda was sent off to the kitchen to begin preparing the meal, though she would obviously have preferred to linger in the bar and chat to Mason.

Juan Jesus opened a bottle of imported Rioja and they sipped as they talked, their voices rising higher and higher to combat the noise of the lashing rain and the cracks and booms from the black sky. The three-legged mongrel sat cowering under one of the tables, occasionally limping into the kitchen to be comforted by his mistress.

Juan Jesus pushed three of the small tables together and covered them with a white cloth. In the centre he placed a candle-holder and lit a tall red candle, his timing being impeccable as at that very moment Linda emerged from the kitchen with the paella.

As they ate and drank more wine, they talked of Los Angeles and Mason's new job; they talked of London and of Jackie's impending first day at the recording studio, and of Linda's middle-class upbringing in Surrey. And Juan Jesus talked on and on, extolling the virtues of Cordoba, Sevilla and the Alhambra of Granada.

Linda scraped a long wooden spoon through the paella, scooping up the remains of the saffron rice, and was about to load it onto Mason's plate, when a sudden gush of water burst through the roof and onto the table.

"Ostia!" cursed Juan Jesus as everyone leapt up and dragged the covered tables across the bar.

Linda rushed to the kitchen to grab a bucket which she placed under the leaking roof. She returned to the table and calmly asked, "More paella, Mason?"

The afternoon passed quickly into the evening and Juan Jesus's speech became more and more slurred from the effect of too much Rioja. He remained jolly throughout, slapping Mason on the back from time to time, and hanging a limp and heavy arm round Jackie's neck. Linda looked on amused to see her husband in such a happy mood.

"He spends too much time alone," she said. "He needs people. Unlike me. He should never have settled here on La Luna. It's too quiet for him."

"But not for you?" guessed Mason.

"But not for me."

"I know it's beautiful here," said Jackie, "but I don't know how you can spend day in and day out, without seeing any new faces. It would drive me mad."

"It has its compensations," Linda informed her. "No robbery, no mugging, no violence, no traffic . . ."

"No life," concluded Jackie.

Linda smiled. "It's the *perfect* life for me."

Avoiding the drips that were now coming through several spots in the roof, Juan Jesus placed a large mattress on the bar floor and handed some pillows and blankets to Mason and Jackie.

"I'm sorry we haven't got a spare bedroom for you," said Linda. "We don't often have people to stay." She laughed. "What am I saying? We *never* have people to stay."

"After the way we've been sleeping for the past two days," replied Mason, "this'll be luxurious. Thanks."

Juan Jesus staggered off to bed attempting to sing an old flamenco song and Linda followed him laughing.

Mason and Jackie, now beginning to feel cold, snuggled under the blankets and hugged each other.

"They're nice, aren't they?" said Jackie.

"Very," replied Mason. He lowered his voice to a whisper. "She's really quite attractive. I can't honestly see what she sees in him."

"Can't you?" asked Jackie, surprised. "I can. He's great fun."

"Not as much fun as me though, is he?" said Mason, snuggling up closer, holding her tighter.

"No," she giggled. "And *she's* not as attractive as *me*, is she?"

"Nobody is as attractive as you," he said, sounding very serious. He kissed her. Then he leaned back, brushing her hair away from her forehead and looking closely into her eyes. "The windows to the soul," he said. "They'll tell me everything I want to know."

"What do you mean?"

"Your eyes will tell me what you really think of me. How *much* you think of me."

"You *know* how much I think of you," she whispered.

They lay silently, looking into each other's eyes.

"You know that message I put into the bottle?" Mason said finally.

"Asking for someone to come and rescue us?"

"I didn't ask to be rescued," said Mason. "I simply wrote, 'MASON LOVES JACKIE'. I want the world to know, you see."

Jackie began to tremble.

He held her even more tightly. "I love you, Jackie," he said.

"I love you too, Mason," she replied softly.

14

Although the worst of the storm had passed, the sea was still choppy and Mason clung onto the rail, his head over the side of the boat.

"Ohhh . . .," he groaned as he took a two-minute rest, with Jackie gently stroking his white forehead. "It must've been that paella."

"Of course it wasn't the paella," grinned Jackie. "I ate it too and I'm fine. It's sea-sickness, Mason, that's all."

"But I'm never sea-sick," he moaned as he returned to the rail.

"There's always a first time," she said, almost to herself.

They were the only passengers on the boat, which arrived thirty minutes late at the port of Lacruz. Nothing else seemed to be moving that day.

"Where is everyone?" asked Jackie as they leapt onto the quay.

"Only a fool would go out on a rough sea like

that," replied Mason. "I'm not surprised there's nobody about."

Jackie couldn't believe the fuss he was making. She hadn't felt the slightest bit sick and had quite enjoyed the way the boat rose and fell on the water.

As the taxi neared the Maritimo, the colour began to return to his cheeks.

"I'm sorry," he said. "I'm OK now, but I've never felt so ill."

She laughed. "My mum always says that men are such babies."

"I'd better leave you here," suggested Mason as the taxi pulled into the hotel. "I'll have to find David and tell him what happened. He'll probably halve my fee for going missing."

"I'm sure he won't," she said, kissing him on the cheek.

"I'll see you later," he called from the window as the taxi made a U-turn and headed back to the main road.

Jackie went to the reception desk to ask for her key, just as Caroline, hand in hand with Glen, entered from the pool area.

"Jackie!" she screeched. She rushed across to her friend and flung her arms round her. "I've been so worried."

"We've *both* been worried," added Glen.

"David Brinkley said you'd be just fine, that there'd been a storm or something on this island where you and Mason had gone . . ."

"I'm fine," smiled Jackie. "Honest. I'm more than fine. Everything was wonderful."

"You must tell me all about it," gabbled Caroline. "Glen's just leaving, so why don't we go and have a drink together and you can tell me all."

"I must have a shower," replied Jackie. "I'm covered in salt and sand. I want to wash my hair and try to make myself look human again."

"You look wonderful," argued Caroline. "Your tan is fantastic."

"You look great," agreed Glen.

"Thanks," laughed Jackie. "But I'm going to have a shower before I do anything else."

"I'll come with you," insisted Caroline, "and you can talk to me from the shower. I want to find out all the sordid details."

As Glen left, promising to return within a couple of hours, Caroline put her arm through Jackie's and led her towards the staircase. "He's got to buy his going home presents," she explained. "Have I got a lot to tell you. But I'm not saying a word 'til you've told me *everything*."

Jackie switched off the hair-dryer. "That's better," she said. "I feel like a new person."

"So, he said he loved you?" enthused Caroline. "Were those his actual words?"

"Yes," laughed Jackie. "And that's it. That's the whole story, with no detail left out."

"You sure?"

"Yes."

"You mean you didn't . . ."

"No!" Jackie snapped. "I've told you everything. Now what about you?"

"Well . . ." said Caroline, flopping onto Jackie's bed and looking up at her friend, who was searching in the wardrobe for some clean clothes, ". . . Glen and I are in love!"

Mason returned to the hotel, scrubbed clean and wearing fresh denim: jeans, shirt and jacket. He found Glen standing at the bar and joined him.

"I take it you're waiting for Caroline?"

Glen stared at him. "I don't know how anyone can look so brown," he laughed. "Anyone'd think you'd been stuck on a desert island for four days." He shook Mason's hand. "Are you OK?"

"Couldn't be better, Glen," he smiled. "You?"

"Great."

"How's it working out with Caroline then?" asked Mason.

Glen grinned from ear to ear. "To tell you the truth, mate, I can't really believe my luck."

Mason mirrored the grin. "You and me both."

"I'm going home a day early," volunteered Glen, "just so as I can travel with her." He laughed. "I don't want to let her out of my sight."

Mason suddenly looked glum. "Good on yer," he said. "I only wish it were as easy for me. I'm off to the good ol' US of A on Monday. So I guess tonight's my last night with Jackie."

Glen grabbed the denimed forearm affectionately. "Then you'd better make it a night to remember, hadn't you?"

*   *   *

La Ronde was the most exclusive restaurant in Santiago, out of financial reach of Jackie and Caroline, but as they'd waited for the girls to arrive at the bar, both dressed to the nines for their last night out on Lacruz, Mason and Glen had rung and made a reservation.

"We could've all sat together," said Caroline, as they arrived and were shown to their separate tables. "It would've been a laugh."

"We'll all get together after the meal," replied Glen. "I think that Jackie and Mason would appreciate taking their last supper alone. And anyway, aren't I laugh enough for you?"

She hugged him. "Of course you are."

Jackie and Mason's table was tucked into a dark corner of the restaurant as Mason had requested. He raised his glass to her, above the flickering candle-light. "Here's to you," he said.

She raised her glass too. "And here's to you."

"It's just a pity we can't say, 'Here's to us'," he whispered sadly.

"You will write, won't you?" she said. "I couldn't bear it if I thought I'd never hear from you again."

"Of course I'll write. And I'm sure I'll be back in London from time to time. Anyway, you'll be taking your next holiday in Los Angeles, surely?"

She smiled. "Maybe."

"And possibly, in a few years' time, I can come to your wedding. Meet the man of your dreams."

She couldn't hold back. "*You're* the man of my dreams, Mason," she sighed. "I can't imagine there'll ever be anyone to take your place."

The waiter arrived with the menus.

"What do you fancy for the first course?" grinned Mason. "Fish?"

Being a Saturday night, Fantasma was crowded. On the dance floor a special foam-party was taking place and many of the customers, knowing what to expect, were dressed in t-shirts and shorts. Most were barefooted. The screams and whoops of delight as the bubbles poured from the foam machine, covering the whole dance floor, did not entice the four lovers into joining the fun. They took a large table on the second floor and Mason ordered drinks at the bar.

"Did you see who's here?" Caroline asked Jackie, as soon as Glen had gone to help Mason with the order. "Duane Sheldon. And he's alone. No bimbette on his arm for a change."

Jackie looked at her strangely. "What are you saying, Caroline? You're not going to let Glen down, surely?"

Caroline grabbed Jackie's hand. "Jackie! I've told you! I'm in love. It's no joke, you know. I wouldn't ditch Glen for anyone, let alone that mindless pop singer."

Jackie smiled. "I'm sorry, Caroline. it's just that—"

"I know. I know how I've behaved in the past. But that's all over now, Jackie. Really. This is definitely the real thing. And I think it's for keeps."

Glen and Mason returned to the table with the drinks.

"I see Mr Music is here," said Glen flatly.

"They're all here, so it seems," added Mason. "David, Kristie and the whole crew. Their last night too. Tomorrow will be all packing and goodbye hugs."

Just the thought of a goodbye hug with Mason made Jackie begin to tremble. There was a pain in the pit of her stomach, a strange kind of pain that she'd never experienced before. How could life, she wondered, be so cruel? She loved him. And he loved her. And after tonight, they'd never see each other again.

"I'm just popping to the ladies'," she said. She stood.

Caroline had seen the desperation in Jackie's eyes. She knew exactly what she was going through. "I'll come with you," she said.

As they left the bar and headed towards the cloakroom, Duane Sheldon emerged from the men's toilets. He saw Caroline and stopped in his tracks, staring at her.

"Well, well, well," he said. He crossed the corridor to face the girls. "You look even more gorgeous tonight," he smirked, ignoring Jackie. "Are you with anyone?"

Caroline smiled sweetly. "Yes."

Duane put his arms round Caroline's waist and whispered sexily, "Go and wave him bye-bye and spend the night with me."

Still smiling, Caroline whispered back, "Take your grubby little paws off me immediately or I'll call my boyfriend!"

It took a few seconds for the message to sink in. Then the deflated male ego with the blond hair attempted, not very successfully, to strut back to the bar.

Caroline closed the door of the ladies' behind her and shrieked with laughter. Several girls adjusting their make-up in the mirrors, turned to see what was going on.

"That told him!" said Caroline. "Arrogant little pig."

She saw that Jackie had covered her face with her hands and assumed that she too was laughing. She soon realized that this couldn't be further from the truth. Jackie's body was shaking with sobs.

"Oh, Jackie," groaned Caroline. She took her friend's arm and led her into one of the lock-ups.

Jackie slumped against the partition and let out a howl. "I can't bear it," she said. "I can't stand the thought of leaving him."

Caroline hugged Jackie tightly. "Oh, Jackie, Jackie . . . what can I say? It's just too awful, I know, but—"

"Don't tell me I'll get over it, because I won't, Caroline. I'll never get over it. I'll never forget him and I'll never find anyone to take his place." She wiped the back of her hand across her eyes. Her tears stopped flowing as she leaned her head back on the partition and gave a long, low sigh. "I don't know how I'm going to cope with it tomorrow," she said. "He's coming to see us off at the airport." She attempted a smile. "You'll have to drag me onto that plane."

"By the hair if needs be," said Caroline, as she

ran her hands across Jackie's cheeks, wiping away the last of the tears.

"In a straight-jacket, more like!"

"Don't worry, Jackie," said Caroline. "I'll look after you. You'll be OK. I promise."

Both girls hugged and hugged.

"It's been a fantastic evening, Mason," said Jackie. "Thanks."

The foursome had returned in a taxi to the Maritimo where Glen had parked his car.

"You can let the taxi go if you like, Mason," suggested Glen. "I'll run you back to your villa on the way home. After we've had a little night-cap with the girls, of course."

He winked at Caroline, who laughed.

"No nightcap," she said. "Jackie and I have got to pack. And so have you, Glen, remember?"

"I've done all mine," grinned Glen. "Why don't I help you do yours?"

"Go home!" smiled Caroline. "It's four o'clock in the morning. We've got to check in at ten and there's loads to do."

Mason kissed Jackie. "No big goodbyes tonight," he said. "I'll be here at eight in the morning to run you to the airport." He looked at his watch and smiled. "Hardly worth going to bed is it?"

"You won't oversleep will you?" she asked desperately.

"Of course I won't," he replied. "I'll see you tomorrow, Princess." He climbed into Glen's passenger seat.

Glen leapt in and turned on the ignition. "I've

got to return the car to the airport for eight o'clock, so I'll see you both in the airport coffee lounge at eight-thirty on the dot," he said. "And you'd better be on time," he grinned, "or else . . ."

"Or else what?" laughed Caroline.

"I'll make sure they're there," said Mason.

Caroline blew Glen a kiss as he turned the car round. The two girls watched the tail-lights disappear down the drive then, arm in arm, they climbed the hotel's steps.

Jackie closed *A Stranger Love* and put it into her hand luggage. She lay back on her bed, thinking, her mind drifting to La Luna and the wonderful friends she'd made there. Fearing that if she closed her eyes for one second, she'd drift into a deep sleep, she suddenly realized that Caroline had gone very quiet in the bathroom.

"Caroline?" she called. "Have you fallen asleep in there?"

There was no reply.

"Caroline? Are you all right?"

Still no reply.

Jackie crossed to the bathroom and opened the door.

"Caroline?"

And then she saw her.

"Caroline!" she gasped. "Oh, my God. Caroline!"

Caroline was lying unconscious on the bathroom floor, blood trickling from her forehead.

15

Jackie sat in the waiting-room of the hospital, anxiously staring at the wall clock which was ticking away the minutes. The Maritimo had been quick off the mark, calling a doctor as soon as they'd been informed of the accident . . .

"They have to be careful, I suppose," Caroline had said as the ambulance whisked her and Jackie towards Santiago. "Insurance and all that. They don't want to be sued, do they?"

"Well, it was hardly their fault, was it?" Jackie had replied. "If you can't look where you're treading—"

Caroline snapped, "It was your soap! You're always doing that. If you'd've put it in the rack, I wouldn't have slipped on it, would I?"

Jackie was silent until the ambulance pulled into the hospital car-park.

"How's the head?" she'd finally asked.

"The head's fine. Bit sore, that's all. It's my

ankle that's killing me. I hope I haven't broken it."

. . . It was now seven a.m. and although there was obviously nothing seriously wrong with Caroline, the doctor had decided that she should have an X-ray, just to make sure there were no broken bones.

As the patient was wheeled along the corridor, with her sore foot raised high out of harm's way, Jackie raced to the main entrance where she'd noticed the phone as soon as they'd arrived.

She rang the Maritimo and asked for the number of the house where Mr Wright and Mr Brinkley were staying.

"There's no telephone there," replied the night porter. "But I think they have mobile phones."

"You don't have the numbers of those, do you, by any chance?"

The question was pointless . . . and she knew it. "I'm afraid not."

Jackie put down the receiver and as she walked away from the booth, she suddenly remembered that Pete Bonehead was using one of the rooms in the hotel as an office. She hurried back to the phone and redialled.

"I'm sorry to bother you again, but . . ." The question went through her mind . . . Can you put me through to Mr Bonehead's room? ". . . There's a man who works for Mr Duane Sheldon and he's got a room in your hotel which he uses as an office . . ." she said.

"Mr Watson?"

"Er . . . yes," said Jackie quickly, although

she'd never known his surname. "Pete. Pete . . . Watson." She began to feel greatly relieved. Pete Bonehead would have Mason's number.

"I'm afraid he's checked out," said the night porter.

"Checked out?" she gasped.

"Three days ago. He's gone back to England I think."

Jackie swayed from side to side, mainly through tiredness, but also with a feeling of impending doom.

"Look," she said, "this is very important." She checked her watch. "A Mr Wright will be calling for me at eight o'clock . . ."

"Just a moment," he said. "I'll get a pencil."

"Oh, God!" she sighed.

The night porter returned a few seconds later.

"Mr Wright, you said?"

"Yes. Will you tell him that I'm at the hospital . . ."

"Aah! You are the lady with the bad head," he said, sympathetically. "Are you all right?"

"Foot," corrected Jackie. Then realizing that he would only have known that Caroline had slipped and bumped her head, and not wanting to confuse the issue further, she added quickly, "Yes, yes. I'm OK."

"That's good," he said.

"So . . . will you please tell Mr Wright that there's nothing to worry about—"

"That there's nothing to worry about," repeated the night porter, as he painstakingly took down the message, syllable by syllable.

"And we'll see him in the coffee lounge of the airport as soon as we can."

There was a long pause as he finished taking down Jackie's dictation in his best handwriting.

"Have you got that?"

"Yes."

"It's *very important*!"

"Yes."

She hung up.

He put the note under the desk, looked at his watch and yawned. Tourists! Why did they always treat him like an idiot? He was thankful it was almost seven-thirty. It had been a long night and he was more than ready for his bed. He smiled when Manolo arrived to take over for the day-shift.

"Is she going to be much longer?" Jackie asked the nurse who'd earlier taken Caroline along the corridor to the X-ray department. "We've got to check in at ten o'clock for our flight home."

"Don't worry," replied the nurse, sounding rather irritated. "You'll be at the airport on time."

Jackie felt it was pointless going into details about how they'd arranged to meet someone at their hotel at eight o'clock.

"Look, I know you're really busy," she said, "but I've got to call someone urgently—"

"There's a pay-phone in the main lobby," interrupted the nurse as she walked off towards the reception desk.

Jackie followed her. "Yes, I know," she said, "but it's a hotel that I have to ring, and I don't know the number. I don't even know the name of it, but my friend does. Can I go along to the X-ray department and ask her?"

The nurse tutted, turned on her heels and headed back along the corridor to 'X-Ray', sighing *"I'll* ask her. You wait there!"

Jackie rang Glen and explained that they might be late, due to Caroline's accident.

Glen began to panic. "Is it bad? Look, I'll come to the hospital straightaway."

"No, Glen. Don't," she said. "She's fine. Really. Anyway, you've got to deliver the car at eight o'clock. I just didn't want you to worry, that's all."

Glen looked at his watch. It was seven-fifteen. "Have you rung Mason?"

"I've left a message for him," she explained.

"So, I'll wait for you in the coffee lounge until you arrive."

"Yes. See you later."

Mason thumbed through the magazines in the hotel reception, surrounded by suitcases and dark-brown holiday makers, dressed and ready for their return trip to London. The representative of Caribtours, a pretty and extremely bubbly woman in her mid-twenties, ticked off the names on her clipboard as each of her clients checked in and boarded the waiting bus to take them to Vega Airport.

By eight twenty, the bus was almost full. Miss Caribtours's "Have A Nice Day" smile began to crumble as she crossed to the reception desk to ask if her two missing passengers could be hurried along. Mason reached the desk at the same time and explained that he'd offered to take the two girls to the airport in his Land Rover and that there was no need for her to worry as he'd deliver them on time for the ten o'clock check-in.

As the bus pulled away from the hotel, Mason began to get a little concerned. It was eight-thirty and he was sure that Jackie wouldn't have deliberately kept him waiting for thirty minutes. Instinctively, he knew that something was wrong. Maybe they were still in bed. After such a late night, it was possible that both girls had fallen back to sleep after their early-morning call. But Mason feared it was worse than that. Maybe Jackie had decided that she couldn't bear to say goodbye and she and Caroline had headed for the airport much earlier.

He called to the receptionist, who was just looking through some notes left by the night porter.

"Could you check room twelve for me please?"

Jackie bundled the limping Caroline into the back of a taxi. Both girls were dripping with sweat, Jackie more so than Caroline. It was obviously going to be another scorcher of a day, but the sweating had been caused more by panic than climate.

"The Maritimo!" Jackie informed the driver. "As quickly as you can, please. We're very late." She looked at her watch. Eight-thirty.

"I'm so sorry, Jackie," said Caroline.

Jackie squeezed her friend's hand. "Don't worry. Are you all right?"

"Fine."

The X-ray had shown there were no broken bones, though the doctor had suggested that if Caroline waited until one of the nurses was free, the badly-sprained ankle could be strapped up properly.

"Thanks," replied Caroline, "but we've got to leave *now*."

The doctor shrugged as he watched her limp off down the corridor to find Jackie.

"There's no reply from their room," said the receptionist. "And their key is here, so they must have checked out."

Mason didn't reply. He ran across the hotel lobby, leapt down the steps and hurtled across the car-park to the Land Rover.

The receptionist continued to check through his notes and found a message for a Mr Mason Wright.

"They said there was nothing to worry about," said Glen. "But it's a quarter past nine. They're cutting it a bit fine aren't they?" He drained back his third cup of coffee. "They've got to go back to the hotel because their luggage is still there."

"You ring the hotel," said Mason. "Tell the receptionist that if the girls turn up, they're to stay there until I arrive."

"Right."

"I'll drive to the hospital. It's not far."

He hurried from the airport's coffee lounge, glancing at his watch. Nine-fifteen. He'd have to really put his foot down.

"He's not here!" said Jackie, panic rising in her voice. "He's not here, Caroline!"

"He's probably gone to the airport," replied Caroline. "Don't get in a flap."

Jackie asked the receptionist for the room key. "I left a message for Mr Wright," she said. "Do you know if he got it?"

"Was this the message?" he asked, calmly handing over the note.

"So he hasn't been here?" She turned to Caroline. "He hasn't been here, Caroline!"

"Of course he has!" said Caroline. "He wouldn't let you down. He probably didn't enquire at the desk to see if there were any messages."

Jackie's eyes filled with tears. "Do you think so?"

"Of course. He'll be at the airport."

Jackie turned back to the receptionist. "Could someone help us with our luggage?" she asked. "My friend has a bad foot."

"Of course," he replied as he pressed a buzzer to summon a porter.

"And will you order a cab please to take us to the airport?"

As the girls climbed into the cab, the receptionist picked up the phone. It was Glen.

"They've just left for the airport, sir," he said.

* * *

168

Mason grabbed the first nurse he came across and enquired in Spanish what had happened to the two English girls.

"I'll just go and check with the doctor," she replied. "But I think they're still in the X-ray department." She plodded off slowly down the hospital corridor. Mason looked up at the clock. It was almost a quarter to ten.

"Thank God," sighed Glen with evident relief. He kissed both girls. "I didn't think you were going to make it."

Jackie's mouth was dry. Despite her tan she was beginning to pale. "Where's Mason, Glen?"

He began to tremble, feeling guilty that he hadn't been quick enough in ringing the hotel.

"He's at the hospital," he almost whispered.

"What?" said Jackie, horrified.

"I rang the hotel to tell you to hang on, but you'd just left."

Jackie burst into tears.

Caroline put an arm round her. "Don't worry," she said. "He'll get here."

"Caroline," said Glen softly. "It's ten o'clock. We've got to check in."

"No, no no no no!" sobbed Jackie. "I'm not going to see him, am I? I'm not even going to be able to say goodbye." Her heart was breaking. She stared through watery eyes towards the airport's main entrance, groaning, "Oh, Caroline, I love him. I love him so much and I'm not even going to be able to say goodbye to him. I can't bear it."

A table-cleaner looked across at the sobbing,

almost hysterical young girl, before averting his gaze in embarrassment.

"They've left?" yelled Mason. "Why didn't you say so in the first place?" He looked up at the clock, sighed deeply and then slumped into one of the waiting-room chairs, his head in his hands, tears streaming down his face, knowing that it was too late.

"Our flight's boarding now," said Glen as he looked up at the indicator. "I'm sorry Jackie. I really am."

"I'm not going," sobbed Jackie. "I can't just leave. I must see him."

"Jackie," said Caroline sadly. "Come on. You've got to go. There's nothing you can do about it."

Jackie stared into Caroline's face. "It was just a holiday romance, wasn't it? It happens to lots of people."

"I think it was a bit more than a holiday romance, Jackie," Caroline replied softly. "But yes. It does happen to lots of people."

"I'm sorry, girls, but we've got to go through customs now," Glen informed them. He gently put his arm round Jackie and led her towards Passport Control. Caroline, hobbling behind them, looked back over her shoulder hoping beyond all hope that she'd see Mason dashing across the airport, calling Jackie's name.

Mason climbed into the Land Rover and stared blankly through the windscreen.

"What am I doing?" he said aloud. "What *am* I doing? Life's too short!"

He picked up the mobile phone and called David Brinkley.

The plane was only half-full, though Jackie didn't notice. She caressed Pedro's beautifully carved instrument, gently resting in her lap and looked through the window at nothing in particular. She saw Mason running along the beach in his yellow trunks and watched him daub the red dust all over his body. She heard him whisper, "I love you, Jackie and I want the world to know." She felt his arms round her and the warm, tender kiss on her lips. And she looked down through her tears at the flute and remembered asking, "How can you bear to lose something you love so much?"

Caroline sat across the aisle with Glen, though she *had* offered to sit in the empty seat beside Jackie. She gripped Glen's hand tightly, wishing that her best friend could be as happy as she was. And her thoughts drifted to London and to the long winter ahead and to her new job. And as a cold shiver ran up her spine, Glen put a comforting arm round her.

"Is this seat taken?" he asked.

Jackie lifted her head to face him.

"Mason?"

"What's the point of going to LA?" he grinned. "I love you, Jackie. And I'm coming with you."

*   *   *

A disembodied voice announced, "Please extinguish all cigarettes . . . and fasten your seatbelts."